THE WALL

Business associates Kerron, Chang and Forrest, three of the richest men on Earth, are old and approaching the end of their days. Desperate to prolong their lives, they seek the man who seems to have the secret of immortality: the mysterious Brett, an adventurer who has apparently lived for centuries. But Brett hides a dark secret . . . and for him to help them, they must accompany him on the most dangerous journey — to the centre of the Galaxy — beyond the Wall!

E. C. TUBB

THE WALL

Complete and Unabridged

LINFORD
Leicester

First published in Great Britain

First Linford Edition
published 2009

British Library CIP Data

Tubb, E. C.
  The wall. - - (Linford mystery library)
  1. Immortalism- -Fiction.
  2. Science fiction.
  3. Large type books.
  I. Title II. Series
  823.9'14–dc22

ISBN 978–1–84782–942–9

01|16

Published by
F. A. Thorpe (Publishing)
Anstey, Leicestershire

Set by Words & Graphics Ltd.
Anstey, Leicestershire
Printed and bound in Great Britain by
T. J. International Ltd., Padstow, Cornwall

This book is printed on acid-free paper

1

Three old men

The night was brilliant with stars. They glittered from the cloudless sky like a handful of diamonds thrown by some careless jeweller against the soft velvet of the night, and like diamonds they were bright and hard and cold. They stared down from the bowl of the heavens with cruel, mocking eyes, and the faint light from their scattered vastness threw tenuous dream-shadows from the worn mountains of an ageing Earth.

Kerron stared at them, feeling the chill of their bright challenge knot his withered muscles and yet feeling the age-old excitement of their mystery accelerate his heart. Fear crawled deep within him; fear of adventure, fear of the great unknown, fear of lost and futile hope and yet these fears were as nothing to his terrible fear of death.

He shivered a little and drew his eyes from the great bubble of transparent plastic sweeping from breast height and covering the entire room. It was warm here, too warm for normal men, and yet the chilly light from the distant stars seemed to penetrate even this high-perched haven of civilized comfort. For a moment he glanced at the thermostat control, tempted to raise the temperature still higher, then a man coughed, and he turned away.

'He is late,' said the man who had coughed. He was a little old man, old as they all were, wrinkled and sere, hairless and with the thin limbs and stringy muscles of a man who has spent too long sitting at a desk. He coughed again, and Kerron shrugged.

'He will come,' he promised. 'Restrain your impatience, Forrest. We have waited long, and can wait a little more.'

'Wait!' The third man of the group snorted and stared at the glimmering stars. 'Why are we here, Kerron? Why did you call us from our comforts to assemble here on the tip of a mountain? Who are we waiting for?'

'A man.' Kerron smiled at the withered form of his friend and turned the thermostat a notch higher. 'One who I think can help us, perhaps the only man alive today who can.'

'Help us!' Fire burned for a moment in the depths of the yellow-faced man's eyes, then died at an effort of inner control. Impassively he folded his arms, and stared towards the heavens. 'I think that you hurt yourself too much, you and Forrest. You have too much hope, too much fear, better be like the elders of my people and accept the fate the gods decree.'

'Stop it, Chang!' Forrest turned on the placid featured man and twitched with emotion. 'You are as bad as the rest of us, perhaps even worse. You are torn between the lust of living, and the conviction that you should accept your destiny with placid calm. Be honest with yourself man! Rid yourself of superstitious nonsense and face reality. We, all three of us here, want to live. We want that with a power nothing can restrain, and if there is a single hope anywhere in

3

the universe that the impossible can be accomplished, then we will take that chance.'

'Steady, Forrest,' warned Kerron, 'remember your heart.' He smiled at his friend's sour expression, and glanced at his wrist. 'He is late,' he muttered, and for the first time looked anxious.

'How do you know that he will come?' Chang glanced at the instrument strapped to his thin wrist, and then at the blazing stars. 'Do I know for whom we wait?'

'Perhaps, he is a free adventurer, a trader on the outer rim, a man who seems to care for nothing and who will admit to no master. His name? Brett.'

'Brett!' Forrest turned to glare at the old man seated at the wide desk. 'That man?'

'You know him?' Chang carefully shook a small blue tablet from a phial and gently placed it between his lips.

'I do.' Forrest sounded grim and displeased. 'I had dealings with him once, a long time ago now it must be. A tall man, slender with long smooth muscles and an unexpected strength. A black-haired man with a cold hard face and eyes which have a yellow gleam — the gleam of gold.'

He shrugged and licked his thin lips.

'He will do anything for money, anything. I remember . . . ' He stopped and shrugged again. 'What does it matter now?'

'I have heard of the man,' admitted the Eurasian. 'I heard of him when I was a mere youth, and . . . ?' He stopped, his eyes wide with unspoken questions. Kerron nodded, and smiled at the startled expression on Chang's yellow features.

'Exactly my friend. You heard of him when you were a mere youth — and how long ago was that?'

In the following silence the unsteady breathing of the three men seemed strangely loud. Chang sighed, and slowly relaxed into the depths of his chair. Forrest grunted, seemed about to speak, and then shrugged and sat poised on the edge of his chair watching the man behind the desk with bright bird-like eyes. Kerron coughed and papers rustled as he opened a thick file.

'I don't know how much each of you has spent on the study of longevity, I can guess by my own expenditure that it must be a major part of your income, perhaps even more. Some little we have learned, and had we united sooner, perhaps we could have learned even more.'

'There are some things of which even friends do not speak,' murmured Chang softly.

'I understand, and I am as much to blame as either of you.' Kerron sighed as he leaned back in his padded chair.

'It was by sheer chance that I stumbled on to your secret, and the discovery turned us from business rivals into close friends. We each know the other's weakness, and knowing it, also know that neither of us has anything to fear from the other.'

'That is past history now,' grumbled Forrest. Older than the others he seemed more impatient, more nervous, as if he had less time for the delicacies than others. Kerron smiled.

'My spies found me your secret, the

thing which you had always feared to admit, even to yourselves. My scientists worked along the same lines as yours did, but perhaps because of an earlier start, learned more.' Kerron leaned earnestly over the wide desk. 'We have followed a dream, an illusion, and we are at the end of scientific hope.'

'No!' Forrest sprang to his feet, one hand clutching at the region of his heart. 'No it can't be! You lie!'

'Do I?' Kerron gestured the excited man back into his chair. 'How old are you, Forrest? You need not answer, I know. You are almost two hundred years of age, Chang is one hundred and fifty and I am about the same. We are, perhaps the longest lived men on Earth, but we are all of us dying. How much longer have we to live?'

'Does it matter?' Chang smiled impassively but a little muscle twitched for a moment high on one cheek. Forrest said nothing, but stared at his trembling hands.

'Once perhaps it wouldn't have mattered, but life is a peculiar thing — the older a man is, the sweeter it becomes. Once, long ago in the history of man, the normal life expectancy was in the region of half a century. Over the years that life expectancy lengthened, more food, better diet, better medical care and attention, improved drugs, a thousand things all contributed to an increased expectancy of life. Seventy years, ninety, a hundred. Remember, gentlemen, I am talking of the average life expectancy, we have very good records to work on, the insurance companies made extremely accurate charts and graphs and could tell to a fine degree just how long any group of men could expect to live.'

'What does all this tell us?'

'Perhaps nothing, Forrest, but our search had to start somewhere, and where better?'

Chang stirred in his chair. 'These researches proved nothing?'

'Nothing.' Kerron thrust at the thick file before him. 'The longevity serum was discovered about a hundred years ago, it increased the normal life expectancy to almost double, a man now can hope to have an active life of more than a hundred years, but it isn't enough. It isn't enough!'

'Perhaps they will discover something else?' Forrest tried to keep the hope from his voice and failed. He glared defiantly at the others, his little eyes hot and angry. Kerron shook his head.

'The very nature of the longevity serum makes it a one-shot treatment. A man can retard his catabolism to a certain degree, but he cannot prevent it, and he cannot renew old and withered tissue. No, my friends, the longevity serum is not the answer.'

'Then what is?'

'I don't know,' Kerron said slowly. He glanced again at the instrument strapped to his left wrist. 'I had hoped . . . '

'The man, Brett?' Chang nodded. 'I begin to understand.'

'I examined every birth record of every man born within the past thousand years.' Kerron rifled the papers of his file. He seemed to be talking for the mere sake of making sound, and deliberately kept his eyes away from the burning splendour of the distant stars. 'I traced every long-lived family, every mutant off-shoot, I repeated a thousand diets and ten thousand combinations of chemicals. I examined the possibilities of the ancient religions, and I even delved into black magic.' He smiled a little self-consciously.

'You found nothing?'

'Nothing, Chang. Nothing — or rather . . .'

'Brett?'

'Yes.'

'That man!' Forrest twisted in his chair, and his thin lips writhed as if he were about to spit. 'That thief? What can he do for us? I know him I tell you, a rogue, a money-hungry free adventurer, we can do without him,'

'Can we?' Kerron thrust aside his papers and stared at the old man. 'You remember him don't you, Forrest? Tell me, how old was he when you met?'

'Old? How can I remember that — now?'

'Let me put it in this way,' Kerron urged gently, 'Was he an old man?'

'No.'

'A young man, then, a boy?'

'No.'

'Middle-aged?' Kerron laughed softly as he stared at the old man. 'Come, Forrest, surely you must remember something?'

'He wasn't old,' muttered Forrest reluctantly, 'and yet he wasn't young. I didn't feel comfortable with him, it was as if there was something unnatural about him, as if he were an old man in a young man's body, or a lad in a man's.'

'I see,' Kerron turned to Chang, 'and you, when was it that you heard of him?'

'I told you, when I was a mere boy, over a hundred years ago.'

'I can see what you're getting at, Kerron,' snapped Forrest, 'but it proves nothing. Brett could have taken the serum, and in any case he's no older than we are.'

'No, Forrest, you are wrong. Brett has never taken the serum, the records are very complete and very strict. I have the retinal pattern of every person who has been treated, and his isn't among them.'

'It must be!'

'It isn't!'

'Could there have been a mistake?' Chang leaned forward, his breath hissing slightly between his lips. 'The retinal pattern, could he perhaps have forged it?'

'Impossible!' Kerron rifled among his papers and lifted a thin plastic card. 'Brett had to register for an independent licence as a free trader. He registered more than one hundred and seventy years ago. This is his retinal pattern, and remember gentlemen, that was before the serum had been discovered!'

'I see!' The Eurasian slowly sank back into his chair. 'Then you think . . . ?'

'Is there any doubt?' Kerron thrust aside the thin plastic sheet. 'We have concrete proof that Brett was a grown man before any of us here were born. He is still an active man, a free adventurer operating on the outer rim. I know that he must have the answer, I know it, and I intend finding out what it is!'

'Will he tell you?' Chang smiled blandly as he stared at the others. 'A man with a secret of such a nature would perhaps be tempted to retain it.'

'We can buy it!' Forrest twitched on his

chair. 'We can offer him everything he could possibly want. We are rich, the richest men in the galaxy, and every man has his price.'

'I don't think that such measures will be necessary.' Kerron slumped back into the depths of his chair, and adjusted the thermostat. 'I have examined Brett's record, and his is a complex character. Gold has no power over him, despite what Forrest says. Power? A man who has lived as long as he has could have had power if he had wanted it. No. I shall deal with him, and I may succeed where you would fail.' He looked steadily at the others.

'Never forget one thing. Brett may have no idea why he is what he is. I doubt that he knows why he has lived so long, and I doubt whether he could give us his unique gift if he wanted to.'

'Then why bother with him?'

'Because he is our only hope.' Fire burned deep in his old eyes, and for a moment he seemed almost young again. 'Think of it my friends. Immortality! To live forever, to watch the race of man spread beyond this galaxy and out to the far-flung universes lying for them across the gulfs of intergalactic space. Men have no time to do what they need. Death comes all too soon, comes to cut down the hope and aspirations of a race destined to set its foot; on each and every world circling each and every star. What chance have we when our journeying is bound by the span of our active lives? What chance for swift progress when men spend most of their brief existences learning, and then a few short years trying to add a trifle to that knowledge before they collapse and die? We three have our own reasons for desiring immortality, what they are remains our personal secret, but one thing is certain, we will share that knowledge.'

Forrest nodded, and glanced impatiently at his wrist.

Chang smiled inscrutably, the saffron of his skin illumined by the indirect lights, and for a moment looking like some idol from an ancient religion. Kerron stared at him, his eyes darkening with sudden suspicion and doubt. He half opened his lips as if to speak, then abruptly jerked his head back and stared into the heavens.

A new star blossomed among the old. A fierce stabbing point of blue-white fire. A thin quivering whispered through the dome, a trembling of the surrounding atmosphere pressed and torn by the passage of some distant body. The stabbing flame came nearer, and seemed to lengthen to turn from a blinding dot into a thin streamer of livid flame, and as it lengthened it moved passing slowly across the glimmering stars.

Tensely the old men waited in the fastness of their dome.

2

Black bargain

He came with a soft whine of hidden machinery, and stood on the circular platform of the hidden elevator as it rose into the domed room and clicked to a halt flush with the rubberoid flooring. He didn't move, but just stood, straight and tall staring at the three old men.

A tall slender man, dressed in a high collared blouse fastened at throat and wrists. Loose trousers were thrust into high knee boots, and wide crossed belts surrounded his slim waist. A long cloak swept from his shoulders reaching almost to the floor, and his thin harsh features were framed by the glittering metal of a close fitting helmet.

Light sparkled from him, little ripples of ever-changing colour gleamed and flashed from the spun metal of his clothing, turning him into a man of light, and for a moment the three sat and stared at him in silent wonder.

'You are late.' It was Forrest who spoke, sitting crouched in his deep chair his little red eyes gleaming like coals in the soft indirect lighting. Kerron coughed and glanced warningly at the old man. He smiled at the tall figure before them.

'Brett, you received my message?'

'I am here.' Light flashed as the tall man stepped from the platform. He loosened his cloak and flung it over the wide desk, and the three men could see the worn butts of holstered weapons supported by the wide belts.

'You know us?' It was a statement rather than a question and Kerron stared shrewdly at the tall figure of the Free Adventurer.

'Chang, Forrest, and yourself, Kerron.' Brett nodded, his face expressionless. 'I know you.'

'Good. Will you be seated please.'

The tall man glanced at them, at the yellow features of the Eurasian, the hairless scalp of the withered figure in the deep chair, then at the white-haired still upright figure of Kerron.

He sat down.

'I'm glad that you could come,' Kerron said softly. 'We have much to discuss you and I.'

'You sent for me, I came.' Brett stared at the old man behind the wide desk. 'There are few men for whom I would do that, but please make what you have to say brief and to the point.'

'I will.' Kerron leaned across the desk and swallowed as he met the cold eyes of the adventurer. 'I have discovered that you are probably the longest lived man in recorded history. I have proof that you were alive and active over one hundred and seventy years ago — and you have not taken the longevity serum treatment.'

'Well?'

'I want you to tell me how you have managed to live so long!'

'I see.' Brett glanced at the paper-littered desk then at the man sitting across from him. 'Proof you say?'

'Your retinal eye pattern taken almost two hundred years ago when you registered for a licence as a Free Trader.

The memory of my associate, Forrest, and the records and sworn depositions of certain spacemen who both travelled with you and who dealt with you in the past.'

'Proof?' For the first time Brett registered emotion, he smiled and gently shook his head. 'My father perhaps?'

'Retinal eye patterns cannot be duplicated.'

'The longevity serum?'

'No. You have never taken the treatment.'

'So because of that you state that I must be long lived. What if I am?'

'Then you can help us.'

'Help you?' Brett shook his head and rose to his feet 'No. I came because I thought that you had something for me, some business proposition. Had I known what you had in mind I wouldn't have burnt atoms to hear it.'

He swept up his cloak and moved towards the platform. Forrest jerked in his chair, one thin claw-like hand slipping beneath the short jacket he wore.

'Wait!'

'Will you operate the elevator please?'

19

Brett stood on the platform and stared at Kerron. He ignored the advancing figure of the burning-eyed old man.

'I said wait!' Forrest halted a few feet from where the tall adventurer stood, and drew his hand from beneath his jacket. He held a long-barrelled weapon in his hand.

'Listen to me, Brett. Either you agree to tell us what we want to know, or you die. Well?'

'Dead men cannot talk,' Brett said coldly. He didn't move.

'We'll give you anything you want, as much money as you can use, but you must help us. If you refuse . . . ' Forrest gestured with his pistol.

'Again?' Brett sighed and seemed to be talking to himself. 'Must we go through all this again?'

'What do you mean?' Kerron rose from his chair and crossed the room. He pressed down the menacing barrel of Forrest's pistol, and thrust himself between the two men.

'All I wanted to do, Brett, was to ask you some questions. I am prepared to pay for the answers, pay well. I must ask you to overlook my associate's behaviour, blame it on his desperation, and try to understand just how desperate he must be.'

'Pay? What do you consider good payment?'

'Ten million in cash.'

'For the answers to a few questions?'

'I see.' Brett stood for a moment, his cold grey eyes slipping from one man to the other. He noticed the burning desperation in Forrest's hot eyes, the silent pleading of Kerron, and finally he stared at the placid features of the saffron-skinned Eurasian. He nodded, and stepping forward resumed his seat.

'What do you want to know?'

'How old are you, Brett?' Kerron rustled his papers as he sank into his seat behind the wide desk. He dropped some, and stooped to pick them up. Brett smiled a little as he met the old man's eyes.

'Do you have to record this conversation?'

'Why, no, Brett. Why do you say that?'

'Then turn off your recorder, you

switched it on when you bent to pick up those papers.'

Kerron hesitated, then threw a switch on the side of his desk. 'Satisfied?'

'No, but some things must be taken on trust. Continue.'

'How old are you?'

'I am an old man, older than any of you here.' Brett lifted a hand at Kerron's attempt to speak. 'That must suffice for now.'

'I see.' Kerron bit his lip, and glanced at his friends.

'Look, Brett, let's be plain with each other. We, my two friends and I, have for many years now investigated the problem of avoiding death, of extending our lives and the lives of all men. We know that you can help us in this quest, you have the secret, will you tell us how it is that you do not die?'

'For ten million?'

'I knew it!' Forrest twitched in his chair as he glared at the light-limbed figure of the tall adventurer. 'Money! That's all he wants! Money!'

'For as much as you ask, as much as we

own.' Kerron stared at the adventurer, his breath fast and shallow. 'Name your price!'

'The treatment for longevity costs exactly one thousand intergalactic credits.'

'Fool!' Forrest sprang to his feet. 'We've had that, we want more, do you understand? More! Not just a few paltry years, but life everlasting! Immortality!'

'Sit down!' Brett didn't move, he didn't raise the tone of his voice, he didn't even look at the wrinkled old man, but Forrest gasped, hesitated, and almost fell back into his chair.

'I understand what you want,' he said quietly. 'I have seen this hunger before, seen it grow in the eyes of men, grow from a faint wish, to a consuming passion. Too often I have seen it, too often.' Brett stared beyond the three men and out to the burning stars.

'I have watched the eyes of my crews. At first there is respect, a youthful hero-worship and an almost fawning desire to serve. Later there is a mature companionship, a healthy loyalty and manly pride, it doesn't last. I have seen their eyes grow hot with hidden jealousy, burning with the secret desire of unasked questions and eventual hate. I have seen it all too often.'

'What happens then?' Kerron almost whispered the question as he stared at the firm figure of the ageless adventurer.

'Mutiny. Desperate promises and futile bribes. I know what is going to happen, and I change my crews before it does.' Brett touched the worn butts of his twin weapons. 'I do not like to travel armed, but desperation can lead men to do strange things — even to threatening to kill the one man who holds what they want most of all.' He glanced at Forrest, his firm mouth twitching a little with hidden amusement.

'Listen, Brett.' Chang raised his voice a little as he called across the room. 'Twenty million for the answer to one question.'

'Yes?'

'Are you immortal?'

'No.'

Silence filled the room, silence and the

faint quiver of a dying hope. Chang shrugged, and folded his arms.

'Cheating, perhaps, but for the sum named will you answer one further question?'

'I will.'

'How is it that you have lived so long?'

'Twenty million you say?'

'Yes.' The Eurasian slipped a thin book from an inner pocket, scribbled quick figures and pressed the ball of his thumb against a prepared place. 'Here! A certified deposition for the sum named to be paid on demand. It will be honoured at any Intergalactic Bank.'

'Thank you.' Brett took the slip of paper, glanced at it, and then thrust it into a pocket. He smiled, and seemed to relax for the first time since entering the room.

'What is life?' he murmured. 'A building up and then a tearing down. Anabolism and catabolism, a constant never-ending war between growth and decay. Any growing thing must either grow or die, there can be no stasis, no firm balance, growth or death that is life.'

He stared upwards out of the dome and stared at the distant glory of the glittering stars.

'Once, a long time ago, when men first began to play with the released forces of the atom, a strange thing occurred. An atomic pile reached critical mass too soon, it was an experimental set-up and without the usual safeguards which would have prevented any like happening being possible. A single technician was on duty at the time, he was making some final adjustments to the pile, when . . . '

'Were you that technician?' whispered Chang.

'A freak accident,' murmured Brett, he didn't appear to have heard the Eurasian's question. 'A thing which could never happen again, and which should never have happened then. Radiation blasted from the exploding atoms, hard radiation, blasting and penetrating everything in its path. Concrete ran in molten streams, steel and other metal vapourised, men dropped for half a mile in each direction, seared by the blasting heat and radiant death, but the sole technician did not die.'

Brett paused, his eyes staring past the room, past the distant stars, gazing deep into the long-gone past. Peering back down the long and solitary years.

'He did not die,' he whispered. 'They found him crumpled at the foot of the pile surrounded by molten rubbish and the bodies of scarred and blackened men. He was burnt, his flesh scorched and his clothes seared to rags, but he was alive! The radiation had penetrated clean through him. Hard radiation, so hard that to it his body was a pane of glass to the rays of the sun. It had washed through each and every cell of him, penetrated the very nuclei of those cells, penetrated, and passed leaving him alive — but different.'

'How different?' Kerron kept his voice low as he asked the question.

'He was almost immortal!'

'So!' Chang sucked in his breath with an audible hiss,

He leaned forward, his eyes glittering hungrily in the bland yellowness of his face. 'Are you that man?'

'I am.' Brett stirred in his chair, straightening and passing a hand across his eyes. He stared at the yellow features of the Eurasian, then at the forward leaning body of Forrest. Kerron sighed, and stirred papers on his desk.

'What happened?' he asked. 'How did that hard radiation make you what you are?'

Brett shrugged. 'How can I tell? I have my own theories, but what are they? Suppositions, guesses, maybes and perhapses, how can I ever be certain of just why I, of all men, should be what I am?' He shook his head. 'Somehow that penetrating blast of hard radiation must have checked something within my body cells, burnt out the inherent tendency of decay, or perhaps it wasn't that. I know that cells are radioactive, each minute particle of life has within it a tiny speck, perhaps no more than a single atom, of radiant energy. It could be that when that tiny mote dies, exhausts its energy, the cell dies and so the body. I have often thought that the blast of hard radiation I suffered revived each and

28

every radioactive particle, or perhaps I suffered a greater change than any man can guess.'

'Whatever it was, can you repeat it?' Kerron licked dry lips as he stared at the youthful adventurer.

'No.'

'Then we have no hope.' Chang nodded, and folded his arms. 'This is the end of a too-bright dream. Immortality is not for man.'

'How can you know that?' Brett stared at the impassive Eurasian, then at the silent figure of Kerron. 'I know why I am here, I knew what you wanted before you sent for me, I have known what you sought from the first moment you set up your laboratories.' He smiled a little at their startled expressions.

'You gave me money, Chang, here!' He tossed the little slip of paper towards the impassive yellow features. 'I have money, more money than you could ever guess. I came because I thought that you could help me. Do you understand? I want you to help *me*!'

'Help you?' Kerron stared at the

adventurer. 'How?'

For answer Brett rose from his chair and stared upwards out of the dome towards the cold beauty of the stars. Light glittered from the spun metal of his clothing, flashing and rippling with the quiet motion of his breath. He stood motionless, his cold grey eyes wide and unblinking as he looked at the burning fires of the distant stars.

'I have lived too long,' he whispered, 'far too long. I have done too much, seen too much, failed too often. I want to solve the last and final mystery, and then I can die, but until that time I must do what I can.'

Forrest half-rose from his seat, and Kerron silenced him with a savage gesture.

'Out there, deep in the vastness of space, lies the final secret, the one great secret against which immortality is but a childish dream. Deep towards the centre of the galaxy, in the very centre, there it lies, and I must solve it! I must!'

'You spoke of help?' Kerron murmured. 'Could we strike a bargain?'

'How?' Brett turned from where he stood and looked at the old man. 'What do you offer?'

'Everything and anything that you want, in return . . . '

'Yes?'

'You help us find eternal life.'

'I can promise nothing.' Brett stared at them, then swept up his cloak. 'I will not give you false hope, you are asking for something impossible for me to give.' He smiled at them, a sudden gentleness in his cold grey eyes. 'I understand your hunger, understand it too well. This I will say, the answer lies somewhere in space.'

'Then we can find it?'

'Perhaps. The way will be long and hard, and death may terminate the quest at any moment, but this I will say, there is hope.'

'Take us there, take us where you will, but give us life!' Forrest clutched at the tall adventurer's arm. He quivered with emotion, little trickles of sweat running down his seamed and wrinkled features. Gently Brett shook off his hand.

'I will do what I can.' He stared at the

others. 'When will you be ready to leave?'

'Leave? Where to?' Chang wheezed a little, and hastily took a blue pill from his phial.

'To the centre of the galaxy, to the birthplace of creation!'

'Are you insane!' Kerron almost ran from around the wide desk. 'You know that you can't go there, no one has yet managed to go there, have you forgotten The Wall?'

'No.'

'Then . . . ?'

'We will penetrate The Wall.' Brett stared again at the beckoning stars. 'Three times before have I tried, and each time failed, but this time I will not fail. Twice I escaped with a wrecked ship and a demented crew. The third time I tried alone, and battled for days to penetrate that barrier. I failed, a man can stay awake just so long and then he must rest. This time we will tackle it together, and together we will either win through, or we will die.' He stared at them, his cold grey eyes burning in the whiteness of his features.

'Do you value immortality enough to risk the few years of life left to you?'

They didn't answer, but stood, each man intent on his own thoughts, staring at the star-covered bowl of night.

3

Preparations

Lights blazed over the spaceport; signal lights flashing with red and green and blue, studding the high control towers and twinkling from the far-flung perimeter of the great concrete apron. Wide swathes of red marked the various landing points, with ribbons of white fire tracking the field across the darkness. Repair sheds and cargo warehouses, administration buildings and passenger lounges, all were marked and glittering with vari-coloured lights. Against the man-made brilliance the stars seemed to fade and die, to glimmer like pale ghosts in the bowl of the night sky.

Waiting!

They were always waiting, thought Kerron with an involuntary shudder. Out in the distant vastness of deep space, flung like tempting jewels a-glitter with promise and adventure, like cold balls of icy fire, cruel and mocking, hard and terribly remote from all of man's hope and fear. He shuddered again, hunching himself deeper in the warmth of his cloak, and beating his thin gloved hands together. Footsteps crunched on the concrete behind them, and turning, he saw the muffled figures of Forrest and Chang.

'Well?' Forrest snapped the word, thin streamers of vapour rilling from his mouth. 'Has he arrived?'

'We are early yet,' soothed the Eurasian. He glanced at Kerron. 'Is all prepared?'

'I have completed all the arrangements Brett ordered.' Kerron stared upwards to where the twinkling lights of hover-cab slowly descended towards the public landing strip. 'One hundred million placed to the credit of the Geriatic Institute, a third from each of us.'

'I hope that they at least can use the money better than we.' Chang smiled as he watched his breath vapourise the chill night air. 'Aren't they the people who discovered the longevity serum?'

'Yes.'

'At least better they than Brett!' Forrest looked like some old monkey as he stood muffled in his thick cloak. 'I am suspicious of that man, he seemed too eager to help, too ready to admit what he was, I don't like it.'

'Then go home.' Kerron stared at the little man with almost active dislike. 'You have had three months to make up your mind, three months to decide what you want and still you grumble. I am going with Brett, I have made all arrangements and there is no more to be either done or said.'

A siren cut off Forrest's retort. A whining shriek yelling from a mechanical throat and sending echoes from the distant hills. Lights flashed as tardy aircraft scurried away from the vicinity of the field, and from high above a point of blue-white flame sent a low rolling thunder throbbing through the air.

'Brett?' Chang glanced upwards at the growing point of light his breath wreathing about his yellow features as he asked the question.

'It could be.' Kerron nodded as a public announcer began to drone their names over his speakers. 'Let's get nearer to the field, the sooner we leave the better.'

The ship slowed its plummeting drop from the heavens, balanced delicately for a moment on spouting venturis, then settled with mathematical neatness on to the broad landing skids. A port opened and spilled bright light across the still smoking concrete of the landing field, and a man jumped lightly down from the vessel.

He was a young man, with a keen intelligent face and sparkling eyes. He smiled as he saw the three old men, and advanced towards them with long springy strides which brought a sick envy clutching at Kerron's heart. He stopped a few paces from them, and gravely saluted.

'You are Chang, Forrest and Kerron?'

'We are,' said the Eurasion softly.

'Will you board please.'

'Where is Brett?' Forrest glared at the young man suspiciously. 'He was to have met us here.'

'Brett is waiting for you,' said the young man, and by the expression in his eyes Kerron could tell just how the young man felt about his chief.

'Thank you,' he said, and moved towards the ship.

It was a small craft, one of the pattern used for planetary search or as an auxilliary to a mother ship. They sat in comfortable seats just behind the pilot and Kerron watched the smooth efficiency of the young man as he radioed the control tower for clearance, and then gently lifted the vessel on jets of spouting flame.

It was a smooth take-off. A textbook take-off with none of the thundering blast of savage acceleration, the muscle cramping pressure of added weight. Such a take-off was heavy on fuel, but Kerron could appreciate the thought behind the action — old men could not stand the acceleration pressure of high grav flight. Brett must have thought of that.

Through the transparent plastic of the ports he could see the dwindling lights of the landing field, they glittered far below like many coloured stars, and for one wild moment he felt that the heavens were below him, and that the brightening stars were the landing lights of some vast unknown field. He shook his head, and eased himself on the padding of his chair.

'The flight will not take long,' called the pilot cheerfully, 'but if you would care to sleep, I will notify you when we arrive.'

'How long?' Chang sat like a placid image of some pagan god, his yellow skin gleaming in the soft interior lighting.

'Five hours, there is food and coffee in thermo-cans within the lockers beside you. If you are cold let me know and I will adjust the temperature, if you feel unwell, I can assist you.'

'Are you a doctor?' Forrest leaned forward in the chair as he stared at the calm face of the young man.

'I am.'

Kerron nodded and forced himself to relax as he settled back in his chair. Of course the pilot would be a doctor, they were old men, unused to space flight, and

Brett had made a promise. He let his thoughts drift as he sat half-dozing in the warm comfort of the gently quivering vessel. A strange man, Brett. A very strange man. He had offered to help them, but needed their aid in return. One hundred million to the Geriatric Institute. One hundred million to finance a science whose sole object was to discover why men grew old and to find new methods of keeping men active and well for as long as possible.

The longevity serum had been one of their discoveries and they had given it to all for the token payment of one thousand intergalactic credits, a sum a man could earn within a year. Kerron smiled as he thought of the terrible temptation some men would have had to face had they made the discovery. Men would do anything for an extended life span. They would pay more, far more than a paltry thousand; how easy it would be to sell the treatment to the highest bidders.

Easy?

He smiled as little wheels began to spin

within the depths of his brain. A businessman, and he had fumbled with the obvious! Simple arithmetic, simple addition, simple, but how many men would see it that way?

A thousand was a sum every man and woman alive could earn within a year. Even at a small profit, say ten credits, say even one, and how many adults in the galaxy? At one credit profit the Geriatric Institute would have made over one million million intergalactic credits. One billion! A fortune even in this age of high wealth when it was remembered that it represented a net profit, and that was not the end of it!

What would be the rate of increase of a race with an extended life span? A race with room to grow in, new worlds to populate? How much in terms of hard profit would that mean to the Geriatric Institute? Even with a low birth rate it could not be less than fifty thousand million, one child born to every ten couples a year, and those children would be ready for the treatment between the ages of twenty and thirty. Kerron smiled as he mentally totalled columns of figures.

Brett had said that he had more money than they could guess at. Was this the source of his wealth? Still smiling, Kerron sank into the fitful sleep of the very old.

He awoke with a start, and for a moment sat bemused as he stared at the back of the pilot's head, and listened to the muffled thunder of the streaming rockets. Through the clear plastic of the vision ports he could see the glowing ball of the distant Sun, brilliant and eye-hurting with its unmasked splendour. A tiny ball hung mistily against a backdrop of stars, a misty ball with a small clear orb suspended close to one side. Earth! Earth and Luna, they must be well on their voyage.

'Are we there?' He stirred a little and glanced at the watchful eyes of Forrest. Chang slumbered, snoring a little, his breath thick and heavy. The pilot nodded, and gestured towards the large visi-screen before him.

'Yes, we should make contact within the hour.'

Eagerly Kerron leaned forward, staring at the screen, then sank slowly back into his seat, his breath a whistle of admiration.

'Big, isn't it?' The pilot turned and grinned at the old man. 'It was built in space, of course, it could never take off under its own power, too big.'

'Built in space,' murmured Kerron. 'It would have to be, and of course it can never land.' He stared in admiration at what loomed before them on the flickering surface of the visi-screen.

A ship. A great vessel looming like a planetoid, ribbed and overlaid with landing strips and bulging observation domes. A titanic sphere, with two long cones sprouting from opposite hemispheres, cones as long as the diameter of the great central globe itself.

It grew rapidly in the visi-screen and as they came nearer, details became visible. Swollen turrets bearing the snouting orifices of multiple guns. Exit and entrance ports, outlined with light and bustling with activity. Starlight splintered from the dully gleaming metal of the hull, starlight, and something else.

A faint web of lambent blue fire, a flickering dream-light, rippling and coruscating in tenuous sparkles of fitful life. The pilot pointed at it, and grinned.

'See it? That blue haze?'

'Yes,' said Kerron interestedly. 'What is it?'

'A ray screen. Brett developed it, and it renders the ship proof against any attack or accident from wandering meteorites.'

'That?' Forrest laughed curtly and scornfully. 'It couldn't stop a flashlight beam.'

'Why should it?' The pilot shrugged as he concentrated on his controls. 'The beam from a flashlight is harmless, but try and fire energy weapons at the ship, or crash a vessel into it and see what would happen.'

'What would?' said Kerron.

'The entire output of all the defence generators would be concentrated on the threatened area of attack. The screen would solidify, set up a process that would turn any object of iron or steel molten. It would emit a pattern of radiant energy calculated to heterodyne any harmful energy source. If the threatening object were of stone or other matter, then the ship would veer from its path, or set up energy currents to swing the object away from the vessel.'

The pilot bent over his radio and muttered several code words. The lambent ray screen flickered and briefly vanished, gently they slid into delicate contact with the great ship.

A port opened before them, and carefully the pilot guided the ship into the brilliantly lit opening. Metal closed behind them, and a moving track carried the little vessel into an inner chamber. Faint sound began to penetrate the hull, and the pilot smiled as he rose from his chair.

'Ready, gentlemen? The chamber contains atmosphere, shall we go?'

He stood aside as the three old men jumped clumsily from the exit port.

Kerron stumbled, unprepared for the lesser gravity and felt a hand catch his arm. The young pilot smiled as he helped the old man regain his balance, and then led the way towards a bank of elevators. The platform hummed softly as they swept upwards, stopping with a faint click on an upper level.

'I leave you here,' the pilot said. 'If you will get through that door please?' He gestured towards a half-opened panel. 'Thank you.' The elevator platform fell soundlessly back into the depths of the vast ship.

Kerron glanced at Chang, then at the trembling figure of Forrest, he shrugged, and thrusting open the panel, entered the room.

Light blazed around them, harsh blue light tingling the skin and making their old eyes burn with tears and pain. He stumbled over some unseen object and almost fell, a hand gripped him, and a green clad man sat him on a chair.

'Will you all please strip.'

'What!' Forrest peered about him, his hot eyes blinking against the too-bright light.

'Take off your clothes please, all of them.' The man sounded tiredly patient. 'You must be sterilised.'

'No, I refuse!' Kerron struggled weakly against the iron grip of the strange man. 'Why should we?'

'You may carry harmful bacteria, please do as I ask.'

Tiredly, Kerron did as directed, feeling the fierce blue light tingle against his withered flesh. He moved numbly into a shower and cringed at the sudden lash of strange smelling chemicals. Hot air blasted at him, drying his rough skin, and a green smock was dropped around his shoulders.

Burning with irritated anger he waited until the others had completed their treatment, then glared at the calm green-clad man.

'Where is Brett?'

'Waiting for you, will you follow me please.' The man stepped into an alcove, and once again they heard the soft whisper of hidden machinery as they swept upwards.

They stopped beneath a great dome of water-clear plastic, and for a moment Kerron thought with keen nostalgia of his own similar retreat on the apex of one of the Mountains of the Moon on distant Earth. A man turned as they entered, a tall youthful seeming man, dressed in spun metal reflecting a shimmering pattern of ever-changing colour. A slender man with old eyes like wells of night in the whiteness of his features.

Brett!

He smiled at them, then turned again to stare at the burning splendour of the undimmed stars. He seemed to have forgotten them, or rather to have noted and then ignored them as things of no great value. Kerron felt a return of his irritated anger, and he made his tones deliberately loud.

'Well, Brett, what now?'

Slowly the light-limned figure turned and stared at the self-conscious trio. He smiled again, as a man might smile when trying to remember unimportant details, then he moved with a quick shimmer of light and sat in a chair.

'You have been sterilised I see Good. Now we can get to work.'

'I was not in need of a bath,' snapped Kerron tersely. 'I had understood that we were to be partners on this voyage.'

'We are, but the voyage has not commenced.' Brett rose and stared at them. 'Before we can attempt to penetrate The Wall, you must be as physically fit as possible.' He looked at the old man. 'What is immortality worth to you? Is it worth the few years that you have left? Is it worth spending what remains of your life, young again and well?'

'Need you ask?' Kerron stared bitterly at his withered arms.

'Listen then. I shall treat you, treat you as men have never before been treated, an experiment if you like, but one which will give you for a short time at least, youth and vigour once more. I shall press into a brief span all the remaining energy of your wasted bodies, and you will burn your life away, but are the ends worth the means? To penetrate The Wall you must be young again, a false youth, but one possible by my science and by your own acceptance of what must be.'

'You did not tell us that before,' accused Forrest.

'No, but does it make that difference?'

Kerron hesitated, glancing at his companions. He could sense their mistrust, their anger at being misinformed, but to be young again!

He nodded.

4

Gamble with death

A mouse scurried from a trap, hesitated at the opening of a tunnel, and then as it smelt the entrancing odour of food, rushed forward.

Radiation blasted it. A shimmering curtain of vibrant energy penetrating each and every cell of the small furry body. It flashed, died, and the mouse ran up to the bait and began nibbling greedily, apparently unharmed.

Meters swung as delicate instruments checked the radioactivity of the mouse, other, even finer instruments tested the metabolism of the creature and stabbing needles took a minute sample of blood. Still the mouse ate, gnawing voraciously at the succulent bait and oblivious to the surrounding instruments. It ate as though it had starved for weeks, it ate with a desperate champing of its jaws, gnawing

51

and worrying the food before it, its little eyes gleaming like tiny jewels from the sides of its head. It ate, and ate, and ate — and as it ate it starved.

Bones began to show through the furry hide. The fur itself became dull and mangy, dead and lifeless, thinly stretched over a withering skin. The tiny eyes dulled, seemed to become covered with a film of opaque whiteness, and the champing jaws fumbled with their food.

Still eating, the mouse rolled, kicked once, and died.

Brett sighed and straightened from the observation window even as a trapdoor swung and the tiny corpse vanished in a spurt of electronic flame. He stood staring at the humped bulk of the machine before him, and heard the faint click of a slightly different pattern of radiation blasted at a second mouse. A hand touched his sleeve and he turned to face a thin old man almost lost in the soft green of his too-big coverall.

'The usual Brett?'

'Yes.' The tall adventurer stared down at the softly clicking machine. 'We have now reached a pattern where the subject starves to death, starves because it just cannot eat enough to stay alive.'

'It was to be expected,' soothed the old man. 'The radiation has speeded up the metabolism, the mouse actually lives at a higher time rate than normal, and has to eat in minutes what normally would have lasted a lifetime.' He smiled, looking at the humped machine and at others exactly similar lined against the wall.

'We have made progress, Brett. We know what patterns of radiation are helpful to man, we can speed healing of flesh and bone, sterilise skin and internal membrane, and even control to some extent the metabolic rate. I wouldn't say that all this has been wasted.'

'Wouldn't you?' Brett smiled as he turned towards the door. 'How many mice have died, and how many failures for each trivial success? Look at it this way, as I do. Each experiment takes five minutes, twelve an hour, just over two hundred and eighty a day. How many different patterns of radiation have we used so far? We have ten machines, and these experiments have been conducted over a period of more than two hundred years!' He sighed again, and stared at the whispering machines.

'A slender chance, one chance in how many billion? Yet what else can we do? Somehow, sometime, the exact pattern of radiation that once blasted at me will be repeated. A mouse will have the same degree of radioactivity, the same metabolism as I have, and when that day comes, the secret of immortality will lie in the grasp of the race of Man!'

'It could be tomorrow,' whispered the old man. 'It could happen now, or never.'

'No. It must happen, but how many infinite waveforms must we try first? We have tried for two hundred years, we may have to try for twenty thousand, and still there will be fresh wave-patterns to try.' He sighed and shook himself a little, his tall figure sagging with an inner fatigue, the spun metal of his dress shimmering with swiftly changing colour at the tiny motions of his muscles. The old man at his side shrugged, and bit his lip in sudden envy as he stared at the tall figure.

Brett smiled. 'Strange isn't it? I am tired of this continual effort, tired of monotony, of always walking alone. How tired you can never guess, and yet I have the one thing which you and millions like you, want more than anything in the universe.' He stared down at the old man.

'Tell me, why is life so sweet?'

'Why does a starving man want bread?' The old man shook his head and avoided the tall adventurer's eyes. 'How can you know the envy men feel when they are with you, Brett? How can you ever know the hunger for life felt by other men? I want to live, to live forever. Is that strange.'

'No, and if it lies within my power, live you shall.' He dropped a hand on the old man's shoulder. 'You know that you can enter the deep-freeze whenever you wish. You can lie in suspended animation for ten thousand years, and to you it will be as though you have but closed your eyes for a moments sleep, and while you sleep, I shall work, I and others, and you will awake to the gift of immortality.'

'I know that, Brett.' For a moment the

old man's eyes glowed with a strange tenderness as he stared at the tall figure before him. 'I know that you are doing your best, we all know it, but . . . '

'Human nature is hard to combat, I understand.' Brett smiled and gently shook the old man by the shoulder. 'Forget it. Now, how are the three new subjects?'

Silently the old man led the way from the room of soft whispering machines, the machines in which generations of mice lived and died in a never-ending effort to find a hidden radiation, a radiation that meant immortality to all men.

He led the way past great laboratories, past sealed rooms and the mysterious bulk of humped machines. It grew chilly, and Brett shrugged the wide cloak a little closer around his lithe figure. The cold increased, and with it came a glare of blue-white light and the faint smell of ozone. A whisper of sound quivered on the edge of audibility, ghost sound, a vibration more sensed than actually heard. This screaming pulse of ultrasonics sterilising the entire vicinity.

A coffin-like object rested against one wall. An open topped container, filled with a thin blue mist and surrounded by the serried bulk of glistening instruments. Hooded ray projectors stared lifelessly at the blue mist, their elements dark and cold. Men moved quietly about the room, tending the open coffin-like containers against the walls, and continually studying charts and meters. One of them looked up from where he bent over the open vat, and stepped back as Brett approached.

'How is the treatment progressing?'

'As predicted. The metabolism has been speeded and their individual time-sense awareness adjusted to an appropriate norm. The life-energen stream has been on trickle flow for the past twenty hours and is now reaching optimum absorption. Naturally, we have corrected all minor irregularities, and compensated for glandular disturbance.'

'Thank you.' Brett gestured and the man stepped back from the mist filled vat. Together Brett and the old man stared into the blue mist.

A man rested within the vat, naked, lying as if supported by water and yet breathing with a quiet ease. Electrodes nestled against both temples, the base of the neck, the groin, and at the terminal ending of the great nerves. He was an old man, with pipe-stem limbs and withered muscles. His skin looked rough and dry, brittle and of the dead whiteness of extreme age and a sedentary life. A thin mane of white hair drifted about the old seamed features, and looking down on him, the old man shook his head.

'It doesn't seem possible, Brett. How can this man regain his lost vigour?'

'Kerron had about fifty more years to live, fifty years of careful nursing of his waning strength and watching his every effort. I am going to compress those fifty years into less than one. For a while, a brief while, he will be active, active with a spurious youth, and during that time, he will do what I need.'

'Fifty years?' The old man looked his surprise. 'So long?'

'You forget the longevity serum, compared to an earlier age, Kerron is equal to a man of about seventy, he has still several years of life expectancy, and I intend using them to the full.'

For a moment they stared down at the withered old man resting in the vat of thin blue mist. Brett bent and examined the recording dials of the instruments surrounding the vat, and nodded.

'Good. His time sense has already been adjusted, and the life-energen flow is restoring his vitality. All that remains is to restore the flexibility of his muscles and body cells, drugs will soften the hard walls of his arteries and erase the calcium deposits around his joints. With intravenous feeding, massage and glandular extracts, Kerron will be a young man again.'

'For how long?' The old man in his green coverall twisted his lips with sudden bitterness. 'Why are you doing this to them, Brett? Why torture them so? How do you think that they will feel, to be young again, but at the cost of a normal life? They will feel the swift rush of blood through vibrant bodies, feel the untrammelled interplay of thought and action, and all the time they will know the price they pay for that brief return to youth. They will live yes, but in constant fear of premature death.'

'What of it?' Brett swung from the mist-filled vat and moved with long strides out of the chill room and into the plastic covered observation dome. The old man followed him, his too-big coverall billowing as he tried to keep pace with the tall adventurer.

'Can man expect the stars without paying the price?' Brett stared out of the clear plastic towards where the clustered stars of the Milky Way traced a glittering path across the night of space. 'What is worth getting if there is no effort in the obtaining of your hearts desire? Man wants immortality, then man must pay. He must pay with tears and futile hope, with high endeavour, and the sacrifice of personal ambition. Those three old men want to live, want life everlasting, and they must pay for it. Not with money, not with the impersonal wealth of intergalactic credits but as I did, with toil and misery, and pain. They want what I have, and they must earn it!'

'How can they?' The old man stared at the youthful figure with hot eyes, and tried to still the trembling of his lips. 'You can't give them what they want, you don't know the secret of life everlasting. You are a freak, an accident of hard radiation, how can you promise what you haven't got?'

'Look!' Brett pointed towards the thick belt of glittering stars. 'Look out there, deep towards the centre of the galaxy, you know what lies there?'

'The Wall.'

'Yes, The Wall, and what lies beyond?'

'I don't know, no man knows, The Wall is impenetrable.'

'Is it?' Brett dropped his arm and smiled as he stared at the burning stars. 'I disagree. I have sent survey ships to examine The Wall, they have been doing it for fifty years now, and I know the way past the barrier.'

'You do? Then . . . '

'Yes.' Brett nodded and turned to face the old man.

'You begin to understand. Immortality

is a myth, a fable, a legend extant on a thousand worlds. The fountain of Ponce de Lyon, the Gift of the Gods, the magic stone and the rare plant. The Phoenix, the waters of Styx, a thousand legends on a thousand worlds, but are any of them true?'

'Behind any legend there must exist a grain of truth,' said the old man slowly. 'Distorted perhaps, but there.'

'Exactly. Somewhere in this galaxy lies the answer. Ages ago, how long ago no man can even imagine, other races ruled the stars and their ships spread knowledge among the peoples of the universe. Somewhere there is a fountain of youth, somewhere, but where?'

'Beyond The Wall?'

'Where else?' Brett smashed the fist of one hand into the palm of the other. He began to stride about the wide room, his clothing shimmering and blazing with ripples of multi-coloured light.

'I have extrapolated all available information along a line-curve equation-graph, and the answer is the same. I have sifted the legends of half a hundred worlds, a score of alien races, and the conclusion is unavoidable. I have tested twenty theories, examined ten thousand records — and always I get the same answer. The Wall!'

'Then what are we waiting for?' The little old man almost trembled as he clutched at Brett's arm. 'Let's go there and solve the secret, let us go now!'

'No!' Brett shook off the old man's grip. 'I understand your impatience, but that is not the way. As yet it is just theory, a theory which has yet to be proved.' He smiled down at the old man. 'You need have no fear, the deep-freeze will keep you in suspended animation for as long as necessary, and while you sleep the secret of The Wall will be solved.'

'I see, and so you are taking three revived old men with you to penetrate the barrier. Why?'

'I have tried to break through before, twice my crew forced me to return, the third time I myself failed. I need a crew, but a crew with nothing to lose, a crew driven by desperate fear. The three old men will provide that crew once they know that they either penetrate The Wall or die within a brief period, then nothing will keep them from their goal.'

'I see.' The old man looked at Brett with a peculiar expression, and instinctively stepped away from the adventurer. Brett laughed.

'You think I am a monster? A thing devoid of human feeling?' He shrugged. 'Perhaps you are right, but I must use what I can, and these three old men, each of them desperate for life everlasting, will serve my ends.' He smiled as he saw the expression in the old man's eyes. 'Have no fear, I shall serve them as well as I may. I promised them immortality, and if immortality is to be found anywhere in this universe, it will be found beyond The Wall. What more can I give?'

'A gamble,' muttered the old man. 'You have taken what remains of their lives, and promise them nothing but a dream. What if you fail? What then?'

'Then they die,' snapped Brett curtly. 'They die, and I try again.'

'You can afford to, you have time, all the time in the universe.' He peered at the shimmering figure of the youthful adventurer. 'Are men nothing to you? Have you lived so long that human emotion and feeling are alien to your thoughts.'

'*What?*' Brett stared at the old man standing before him in his too-big coverall, and his face hardened at what he saw.

'Even you,' he murmured bitterly. 'After all this time, all these years of working together, you also have turned against me. Once you would have understood, but now you are too wrapped in your own affairs, too greedy for self-gain.' He sighed, his hard features softening a little as he stared at the cringing figure before him. 'It is time for you to rest,' he murmured. 'Notify your assistant to take over your department, and present yourself to the vaults on Calistrana. Rest easy old friend, when you awaken from suspended animation, the galaxy will be yours to enjoy — forever!'

'I'm sorry, Brett, I didn't mean . . . ' The old man faltered into shamed silence.

'I understand, have no regrets, but go. Go now!'

A young, trimly-dressed officer almost ran into the room, hesitated at the sight of the old man, and saluted as Brett caught his eye.

'A message from central observation, sir.'

'Yes?'

'An unidentified ship has been spotted hovering on the edge of our radar screen. The vessel is armed, and does not reply to our signals.'

'Does the vessel betray any hostile tendencies?'

'No, sir. It appears as if it is waiting for something, or someone.'

'I see. Keep normal safeguards, I don't think that ship will trouble us for long.'

Brett smiled as he stared at the stars.

5

Spurious youth

Pain and the searing agony of returning awareness. Pain and the soft mutter of distant machinery, the soft hiss and sigh of pumps, and the tingle of ultra-violet lamps. Kerron moaned and twisted against something hard and cold and smooth. Again came the lancing agony, a thousand needles of electric fire stabbing against tender skin and probing with fiery points the quivering matter of his naked brain. He sighed, grimly forcing himself to keep his eyes tight-shut, determined to sink back into the warm dark oblivion from which he came.

Again the searing thrust of stabbing fire. Warmth flooded him with the invisible infrared rays from hooded projectors. He twisted as he felt the wash and flow of high frequency eddy-currents as they penetrated his every cell, forcing his sluggish blood to race through his arteries.

He muttered, struggled for a moment, and then opening his eyes sat upright.

He was in an open coffin-like vat, a container of some smooth dark plastic surrounded by glittering instruments and hooded with the light-filled bowls of ray projectors. He shivered a little, hugging his naked body, and a man bent over the edge of the vat with a glass half-full of some grey fluid.

'Drink this,' he ordered.

Obediently Kerron drained the glass, feeling a warm glow as the thick grey fluid coursed down his throat. He smiled and held out the empty glass, his eyes automatically following the object. He stopped, the glass halfway towards the young man, and stared at his hand.

Silently the man took the glass, and as silently left the side of the vat. Kerron didn't notice his going, he just sat and stared, sat and stared at his own hand, a firm youthful hand, a smooth, pink healthy hand, a hand he didn't recognise.

Swiftly, his heart thudding against his

ribs, he climbed from the vat and examined his body. He was young again. Young, and with the lithe figure, the smooth soft skin, the rippling muscles of youth! He sobbed a little with sheer happiness, and stood running his hands over his own firm flesh while a thousand questions flooded through his bewildered brain. A sound made him turn, the very action sending fresh waves of exultation racing through his veins as he remembered what he had only recently been, and stared with wonderment at two other naked forms.

Chang he recognised, the Eurasian's skin gleamed yellow beneath the harsh blue-white glare, but Forrest!

He was still bald, and his hairless scalp seemed ludicrous against the comparison of his boyish figure. He stood there, a young man with a bald head, and blinked foolishly in the too-bright glare.

'What happened?' he said, and his voice was as it had once been, strong and loud but still querulous and with a faint petulance. 'Who are you? What happened to me?'

'Can't you understand, Forrest?' Kerron stepped easily towards his friend. 'Brett has given us back our youth. Chang! Forrest! We are young again!'

'Immortality?' Chang shook his head as he stared at the fresh skin of his arms. 'So easily?'

'It must be.' Forrest spoke with a desperate urgency as if to convince himself more than the others. 'I knew that he had the secret, we paid what he asked, and he has made us immortal!'

'No.' Kerron frowned and glanced at Chang. 'I don't think so, do you remember? Brett told us that he would treat us in some way, but that after we were to do something for him, what was it, Chang?'

'I'm not too sure, my memory . . .' The Eurasian closed his eyes, then shook his head. 'Still need we worry? He will tell us what we have to know later, now let us see what we are.'

They had youth, there could be doubt of it. They had health and the soft flesh and firm muscles of their early days when the world was bright and interesting, and the slow march of age hadn't warped their time sense. Kerron walked about the room for the simple pleasure of walking without effort. He breathed deep, deeper than he had done for years, and smiled at the swelling of his chest. He even jumped a little, and felt the sudden urgent need for swift and violent physical effort.

He didn't notice the opening of the door, nor the men who softly entered and stood quietly watching their every move.

'Well, gentlemen, are you satisfied?' Brett strode towards them, his spun metal garments limning his tall figure with rippling light. Kerron spun at the sound of the voice, and smiled as he recognised the tall adventurer.

'Brett! You have given us back our youth!'

'No.'

'Then . . . ?' Kerron gestured towards his two friends and tried to keep the disappointment from his voice.

'A revivifying of your bodies, a compressing of your life expectancy into a brief period.' Brett smiled and seated himself on the edge of one of the empty vats. 'I need not go into details, but you are now living at an increased rate of metabolism, catabolism rather, for you will never be better than what you are at this very moment.'

'Then it isn't immortality?' Forrest cursed with savage violence. 'You cheated us, Brett. I always knew you for a thief!'

'Did you?' Brett smiled contemptuously, and addressed himself to Kerron. 'I need you for a purpose I have in mind, something which must be done, and which you are going to help me do. I explained this before, but one of the effects of revivifying is a slight loss of memory and so I will repeat it. I need a crew for a ship with which I intend to penetrate The Wall. You will be that crew. You will do as I ask because there is a high probability that the secret of immortality lies beyond The Wall. You are at liberty to refuse.'

'Have we an alternative?'

'You may return to Earth if you wish, but I must warn you, you will be dead within a year.'

'Dead!'

'Yes. I have compressed what remains of your life into a brief period of activity. It is as though a low voltage electric light bulb were to be attached to a high voltage current. For a brief period the lamp would burn with terrible brilliance, then it would die, burnt out, and the same thing will happen to you.'

'I see.' Kerron frowned in thought. 'I will go with you. Chang?'

'Yes.'

'Good, and what about you, Forrest?'

'Can I do other?' The man glared at Brett, his lips writhing as he stared at the slender figure sitting on the edge of the vat. 'We appear to have been very neatly trapped!'

'Exactly.' Brett rose and stared at the three men. 'One other thing. A ship appears to be waiting for some form of signal, it hovers just outside our radar screen. Who owns that ship?'

'A ship?' Kerron frowned. 'I know of no ship.'

'Nor I,' snapped Forrest. Brett smiled and stared at Chang. 'Do you?'

'No.'

'Very well then. I shall order the vessel to leave the vicinity or I shall destroy it. Now to business. We leave as soon as you are fit. I have a vessel waiting for us, one specially designed, and speed is important.'

He turned, rising from his seat with a swirl of colour and hesitated at the door. 'For your own good, do not forget that the sands of your lives are running out. From this moment on you are getting older, rapidly older, and remember to act as old men should act.' He smiled at them with a trace of humour. 'You have all had experience in what I mean.' The door swung behind him cutting off Forrest's stream of bitter curses.

'What did I tell you?' He glared at Kerron and Chang. 'Trapped! Forced to do as he orders. I never did trust that man.'

'Have we any choice?' Kerron shivered a little and hugged his arms about his naked chest. 'We knew what we were getting into, and we can't back out now.' He stared at the bald man. 'I don't want to back out anyway. I'm going on until the end.'

'Brett seems to know what he is doing,' murmured the Eurasian. He stooped over a pile of clothing and began sorting out the regulation space wear. 'Immortality isn't to be won by sitting back and relying on others. If we want the prize, then we must get it.' He began to wriggle into his clothing.

'I still don't trust him,' insisted Forrest. 'I don't like the look of him, and have you ever noticed the colour of his skin? White, dead white, and every other spaceman I've known has always been tanned by the free radiations of space. Another thing. Why does he wear that spun metal clothing? I'll bet half of what I own that it's made of irillium, and if I'm right, then his clothes must have cost a fortune, irillium is the only metal known which can be spun so that the threads act as a diffraction grating. Why does he wear it?'

'How do I know?' Kerron snapped the buckle of belt and stretched glorying in the feel of his new garb. 'A lot of men do peculiar things, and remember that Brett is just an ordinary man. If what he says is true, then he must have lived longer than we guessed.'

Forrest shrugged, and stood frowning, lost in deep concentration. He sighed and to Kerron's surprise, grinned at them both.

'Funny about that ship,' he said to no one in particular. 'I wonder which one of you owns it?'

'I know nothing about it,' snapped Kerron sharply. Chang shrugged.

'What would be the purpose of such a vessel?' he said blandly. 'Fate will decide whether we live or die, what use to struggle against fate?'

'Perhaps, and yet should we discover the secret of immortality, think what power it could give a man — or group of men.' Forrest breathed deeply, his hot eyes staring at them both, 'Such a group could own the universe, even the other universes which lie across the gulf of intergalactic space. Think of it! Immortal rulers of an empire so vast that no man can think of it as a whole!' He grinned at them, his mouth slack and for a moment

Kerron thought that the bald headed man was intoxicated. He opened his mouth to snap a retort, then staggered and leaned against the side of one of the vats to steady himself.

His head spun, and his vision blurred as he fought to remain on his feet. Chang collapsed, giggling helplessly as he rolled on the floor, and Forrest laughed insanely as he tried to kick the Eurasian.

They were all intoxicated!

Kerron felt the sweat pouring from his face and neck as he struggled to remain on his feet. He remembered the thick grey fluid, the suspicious way in which they had been left alone. Brett's deliberate curtness as he informed them of what they had to do. He opened his mouth to scream, and shuddered as he heard the senile tittering rilling from his open lips.

He never felt the impact as he hit the floor.

A man cradled his head, and another held a glass to his lips. Weakly Kerron drank, swallowed, drank again. He felt a needle bite into his flesh, and gently relaxed against the supporting arm.

'What happened?'

'Adjustment reaction,' explained the man supporting his head. 'We expected it, but it has to work itself out naturally. You'll be alright now.'

'I don't understand?' Irritably he tried to clear his buzzing head. 'We were perfectly alright, then after a while we acted as though drunk. Why was that?'

'Re-orientation of your altered time-sense. You were living at a conflicting ratio between mind and body. The enzymes of your cellular structure were at variance with the syncope of your neuron paths, the internal conflict resulted in malad-justed synapses and you felt exactly as though you were intoxicated.'

The man smiled at Kerron's puzzled expression.

'Let me put it this way,' he suggested. 'Your body has undergone a complete overhaul, but your mind remained as it was. When you awoke there was a period when your mind and your body couldn't agree, just as if you were both a young man and an old one at the same time. The result was an internal conflict with a derangement of your thought processes, and naturally you felt as if you were drunk.' He lifted the glass again.

'Swallow a little more, you'll be all right now, and the trouble will not recur.' He smiled again as he lifted the glass away from Kerron's lips.

'Did you know that would happen?'

'Yes, that is why you were left alone. The psychological factor is important and you had to settle down without external aid.'

'I see.' Kerron licked his lips and struggled to his feet Chang seeming even more yellow than usual, joined him and Forrest followed close behind. The Eurasian smiled and shook his head in baffled wonder.

'I have been ill before, but never so suddenly and never without any stimulants.' He looked at Kerron. 'What now?'

'You are to join Brett at the ship.' The young man with the hypodermic stared curiously at them. 'When you are ready?'

Kerron nodded and together the three once-old men left the room.

6

Nyeeda

The ship waited on a launching cradle just off the main observation dome, a slender torpedo-shaped craft with flaring venturis and a single turret bearing triple guns. Kerron paused just within the dome and frowned at the panorama above.

'Where's Earth?' He stared at the stars and creased his brows in puzzled wonder. 'Where are we?'

'Well towards the centre, Kerron.' Brett stepped from where he sat at a wide desk and smiled. 'We have not been idle while you were in the revivifying vat. The ship has cut two hundred light years off our journey, but from here we travel alone.'

'Why?' Chang folded his arms and smiled blandly at the tall adventurer. 'Couldn't this vessel take us all the way?'

'It could, but if it got too near The Wall, sub-etheric stress would wreck it. Besides that, this ship is needed elsewhere, we shall travel in the small ship waiting for us.'

'Just we four?'

'Yes.' Brett stared at the bland Eurasian. 'I shall pilot and the rest of you I know are able to handle a spaceship. You will be engineer, Chang. Kerron will sit with me as co-pilot. Forrest will serve as best he can.'

'As engineer?' Chang smiled and raised his eyebrows. 'You flatter me, Brett. Are you certain that I can handle your engines?'

'Yes.' Brett stared at the smiling Eurasian. 'I know that you can, after all, you helped perfect the hyper-drive.'

'Thank you, I shall be happy to assist.'

'Right. Board now, and let's get on our way.' Brett moved towards the open port of the small vessel, and after a second's hesitation, the other three followed him.

Metal clashed, and with a faint hiss of air, the small ship drifted from the great bulk of the mother ship and slowly headed towards the distant void. Kerron stared back at the dully gleaming hull behind them, and suddenly narrowed his eyes at a symbol blazoned on the metal. It was a looped cross, the *crux ansata*, age-old symbol of eternal life and the badge of the Geriatrics Institute. He smiled as he settled back in his seat.

With delicate touches of the firing levers, Brett steered the little craft away from the dwindling bulk behind them. The muted throb of the ion rocket-drive quivered through the hull, and Kerron could imagine the miles-long tongue of blue-white fire lancing from the exhausts at their stern. Interestedly he watched as Brett aligned the nose of the vessel.

'Are we entering hyperspace now?' Kerron stared at the star-studded visi-screen before them and let his gaze rove over the banked instrument dials facing the cushioned pilot's chair.

'Yes. We'll take short hops until I am certain our direction is correct. We have a long way to go, and I don't want to waste time correcting our course.' Brett sounded very curt.

'Does it matter?' Kerron smiled at the hard-faced pilot and wriggled himself more comfortably into the depths of his chair. 'After all, a few light years either way won't make all that difference.'

'No?'

'Well, would it?' Kerron tried not to be offended by the barely-hidden sarcasm in the pilot's voice.

'Listen, Kerron. I know the conditions about The Wall, do you?'

'No,' he confessed. 'I don't really know much about it at all, except that no ship has over penetrated the barrier.'

Brett peered through the eyepiece of an electro-telescope and made a last careful adjustment of the instruments before him. Abruptly he thumbed a button.

'Control to engine room. Ready for hyper-drive.'

'Engine to control,' replied Chang. 'Fire at will.'

Brett smiled at the routine answer and deliberately pressed a short lever, from deep within the vessel a generator whined with increasing speed, the whine rose, became a thin high-pitched scream, rose higher until it quivered and tore at shrinking flesh and cringing nerves, then it seemed to fade away to climb above the limit of audibility and hovered on the threshold of hearing a half-felt unheard vibration.

'Ready?' Brett glanced at Kerron and smiled with a sudden flash of white teeth. Kerron nodded, fighting his ingrained fear and clutching at the padded arms of his chair. Brett thumbed the button again.

'Attention! Control to ship. Entering hyperspace.' Deliberately he threw a switch on the panel before him.

Strain clutched the vessel, a sub-etheric strain as force fought with force, twisting and throbbing throughout the metal structure of the ship. Kerron felt sweat start from his face and neck as his body writhed beneath the impact of terrible stress. For one horrible moment he thought that the generators had failed, that the ship had collapsed, that he was being twisted horribly in some alien dimension, then it was over, and the visi-screen showed the thick coiling grey mist of hyperspace.

He wiped his forehead and forced himself to smile. Hyperspace was an old thing, the hyper-drive had been known and used for almost a thousand years, yet still it remained a thing of mystery. It had enabled men to reach the stars, to blaze a trail across the galaxy, to set the foot of the race of Man on a thousand worlds, and still no one knew just how it worked.

A condition of space strain was created about the ship, a locked intermeshed field of opposing forces. It took power to create, tremendous power, and the field itself could not logically exist in a normal universe. It could not exist, but all space strained to correct the paradox.

The held was a fact, but so also was the inexorable law that it simply could not survive. Natural law strove to abolish the unnatural sub-etheric condition of spatial strain, but all the power of atomic engines strove to maintain the artificial field. It could not exist, but it did, and so the field and all it contained vanished from the normal universe, and went elsewhere,

Just where that was no man knew. It was a region of grey mist, a region where the normal laws of the universe did not apply, and man made use of just one facet of that weird dimension. A ship in hyperspace could travel faster than light. Two hours in hyperspace were equal to three light years of normal distance covered. A strange fact an inexplicable fact but it had made mankind rulers of the galaxy.

Kerron shivered a little as he looked at the swirling mist before him, and tried not to show his fear. Brett swung in his chair, and smiled at the white-headed old-young man

'Gets you, doesn't, Kerron?' He pointed at the writhing grey mist. 'What lies out there? I have travelled across the galaxy many times, but still I do not know. A scientist I met many years ago, an old man even then, had a theory and I have yet to hear a better.'

'Yes?' Kerron swallowed and tried not to look at the screen.

'He made an analogy between the universe and a series of concentric spheres. He said that the hyper-drive permitted a ship to pass from an outer space down to a smaller one. Distance travelled on the surface of that smaller sphere would naturally be increased in relation to the outer one. Like the spokes of a wheel, pass down one spoke, travel around the hub for a short way, and if you rose up a second spoke, you would find that you had moved a great distance around the rim of the wheel.'

'Do you think that he was right?' Kerron was interested, despite himself.

'I do.' Brett sounded convinced. 'When first the hyper-drive was discovered, a ship moved at the ratio of one light year per two hours. Then it improved to one for one, now it is three for two. Your friend, Chang, helped to make the latest improvement.'

'How does that prove your theory?'

'Isn't it obvious? As the drive improves we are able to penetrate nearer to the axle of the wheel, and the faster we go, relative to our own universe, of course.' He stared at the screen and smiled at the pressing grey mist.

'I remember those early days, when the drive was a thing of crudely aligned coils and the supersonic drove men insane on the long hops. Things are different now, but men had to be hard then.'

'You remember those days, of course.' Kerron stared enviously at the tall pilot. 'What memories you must have!'

'Memories?' Brett laughed curtly. 'You are following a dream, Kerron, an age-old dream. You long for immortality, and yet you cannot know for what you ask.' He shrugged as if annoyed, and Kerron hastily changed the subject.

'Tell me of The Wall, Brett. What is it?'

'I don't know, that is I don't know what it is, but I know what it does. In the centre of the galaxy, in the mathematical centre, lies a region beyond which ships cannot pass. A great sphere of repulsive force, a sphere more than a hundred light years in diameter. The surface of this sphere is of a peculiar nature. It is totally reflecting, and it carries light rays one hundred and eighty degrees in a closed arc. You can see what that means, of course.'

'It would be invisible,' murmured Kerron. 'If it swung all rays of light one hundred and eighty degrees you would never know it was there, you would see what lies beyond it, see as though it were made of glass.'

'Exactly, and we would never have known about it but for two things.'

'Yes?'

'The hyper-drive and the rift.' Brett smiled at Kerron and idly checked his instruments.

'Ships stopped at The Wall, which is how it got its name. They couldn't pass it and had to feel their slow and cautious way around it, now it is charted of course, but for a long time ships attempting to cross the galaxy had to make a wide sweep and align their ships by trial and error.'

'I understand that, but what about the rift?'

'A hole in The Wall.' Brett stared grimly at the swirling grey mist reflected on the visi-screen. 'Men had seen it for years, and didn't know what it was. A black smudge on the heavens, a dark spot through which they could see no stars. They thought that it was a cloud of dust particles, and forgot it in other interests. I examined it, and know it for what it is.'

'A hole?' Kerron frowned as he strove to follow the other's line of thought. 'A rift in the force field do you mean?'

'Something like that, words aren't important now, only the fact that the rift is a means of penetrating The Wall is important. It is a place of terrible spatial storms, a focus for eddies of free radiation and sub-electronic stress. There is a tide of energy flowing from the rift, a tide against which a ship has to battle for many days before it can even hope to get through.'

'I see, and we are going there?'

'Yes.'

Kerron swallowed and felt the return of an age-old fear. He had always been fascinated by the stars, by their cold and distant glory, and now he was among them, almost alone and defenceless in the void. He wiped sweat from his face and neck and tried to control the thudding of his heart.

'Are you ill?' Brett stared at him, his eyes hard and suspicious. Kerron bit his lips.

'No, I'm all right, just leave me alone.'

'Space sick?' Brett smiled in swift understanding. 'Better go aft and rest a while, this hop will take some time, and the automatics can handle anything which may happen. Get some rest now.'

Thankfully, Kerron stumbled his way from the control room and, into the small dormitory. Forrest was already sprawled on one of the bunks, and Chang smiled at him from the edge of another.

'Come and join us, Kerron, remember that you're an old man and need plenty of rest now.' He chuckled as he lifted a smoking thermo-can of coffee, and passed another to Kerron.

'Have a drink, it is vitamised, and will chase some of the bogey men away.'

'Bogey men?' Kerron took the thermo-can and pressed in the top, swirling the contents as he waited for them to heat.

'Yes, the things which dwell among the stars, surely you've heard of them? The old spacemen were full of the tales, great monsters which came out of hyperspace, visions appearing at the ports, even the sound of babies crying where no baby could possibly be.'

'Now I understand you.' Kerron laughed and sipped at the hot coffee. 'They were strictly the results of unshielded radiation playing havoc with the neuron paths of the brain. As soon as they perfected the shielding, the bogey men vanished, and a good thing, too.'

'Maybe, but it meant the death of some really tall tales.' Chang grimaced as he tasted the hot liquid. 'I don't know, but being young again has its disadvantages, somehow I don't think that I'd wish for a return to eternal youth, I'll pick good old middle age.'

'Why?'

'Well, what did you do when you were young? Chase a few women, chased a lot of money, worried about not getting on in the world, a lot of immature thoughts and needless running about. Now at middle age your life is settled, you can relax, have a good time, take things easy. I'll pick middle age anytime.'

'I'll take what I can get,' said Kerron, and set down the empty can. 'Sleep now, I'm tired.' Thankfully he nestled into the soft mattress and closed the whisper of the hyper-drive from his aching ears.

A hand woke him, a firm hand pressing on his shoulder, and suddenly alert, Kerron sat up on the narrow bunk Brett stood over him.

'Kerron,' he whispered. 'Get up and come with me.' He looked tired and the unnatural pallor of his features showed clearly against the dim lights and the dulled glitter of his clothing. Hastily Kerron rose and followed the tall adventurer out of the room.

'We have landed,' Brett said quietly, 'and there is a thing which I must do. Arm yourself and follow me.' He waited impatiently as Kerron fumbled with unaccustomed weapons, then led the way through the airlock of the ship.

They were on a planet, a strange place full of the warm scent of animal life and with the fragrance of exotic blossoms heavy in the thick air. It was night, and the ebony sky glittered with the points of countless stars, they spangled the heavens and Kerron looked in vain for the familiar constellations of Earth. Even the Milky Way was missing, and by that he knew that they must be well towards the centre of the galaxy.

For a while they walked in silence, Brett moving with sure swift feet, and Kerron stumbling along behind. Light grew before them, light and the noise of many men. A shack loomed against the stars, and then a clutter of rough dwellings, A boom town or a trading post, common on the thinly-populated worlds lying off the main space lanes.

Brett halted outside the wooden door of a low-roofed building and turned his white face to Kerron.

'Follow me, and do nothing except at my command.' Abruptly he threw open the door.

Noise lashed at them, noise and the thick drifting clouds of pungent smoke from native tobacco. Men stood clustered around a bar, other men sat at little tables, intent on various games of chance. A piano stood on a low dais, its stool vacant but with the signs of recent occupation. The door banged behind them, and Brett headed towards the bar.

As he moved, light glittered from his cloak, and silence seemed to follow him like a wave of threatening hostility. A dirty scar-faced man lurched up to them, his breath foul and his eyes glittering with a strange hot rage.

'What do you want?'

'A drink.' Brett slammed his hand down on the rough wooden bar and gestured impatiently towards a surly bar tender.

'Yes?'

'Drinks, and be quick about it.' Abruptly the tall adventurer spun and grabbed the scar-faced man by the collar of his filthy shirt. 'Where is she?'

'Who?'

'The piano player, Nyeeda, where is she?'

Deliberately the man spat and shrugged. 'Who cares?'

The sound of flesh striking flesh sounded strangely loud and in the sudden hush the scar-faced man picked himself from the dirty floor, blood rilling down his twisted features.

'I asked you a question,' Brett said

coldly. 'I want an answer. Where is Nyeeda?'

'That — !' The man spat again. 'If you want her find her, you can have her for me.'

'Fetch her.' Brett stared at the man, his white face expressionless. 'Fetch her now!'

Something in the eyes of the adventurer stopped the crude answer, and with a sudden stream of curses the man shuffled his feet and left. Grimly Brett stood at the bar, one hand within the shielding confines of his glittering cloak, the other holding his untasted drink. Gradually the sounds of normal life returned to the bar.

Kerron stood just behind the adventurer's tall figure and wished that he were safely back on Earth. He tried not to grip his gun-butt, such a gesture could lead to sudden and violent action, but he longed for the comfort of the deadly weapon.

Together they stood, two strangers in a strange environment, waiting.

A woman walked through the crowd, a tall woman, no longer young, and yet with the traces of a once remarkable beauty still apparent on her face and figure. She walked as though she trod on dirt, carefully avoiding even the casual touch of another's garments, and her expression was one of utter indifference. She halted before them, and as she faced Brett her expression changed.

'Brett?' She whispered the name, her delicate brows arching in disbelief. 'Is it Brett?'

'It is.'

'So you remembered?' She smiled and at the sight Kerron felt his throat catch at her beauty. 'I have waited so long for you to return, so long. I had almost given up all hope, but you promised, and somehow I don't think that you ever broke your word.'

'I have never broken my word,' agreed Brett. He swayed a little, his arms moving as if to clasp her tightly to him, then as if remembering something, he stepped away. 'Are you ready, Nyeeda?'

'Ready? Yes, I am ready, I have been ready for so many years now, but I stayed here, I had to stay here, for if I moved where would you find me?'

'Nyeeda,' Brett whispered. 'Nyeeda!'

For a moment they stood almost face to face, and Kerron could sense the tides of emotion straining at the impassive figure of the tall adventurer. On the edge of the watching crowd a man moved in sudden motion, and even as Kerron called a warning, Brett acted.

Light swirled and glittered as he swung his cloak, shielding the woman in its heavy folds. A lance of searing energy blasted from the man at the edge of the crowd, and with sudden abruptness, the room was clear as men dived for cover.

Kerron stood, half-deafened by the thunder of the weapon, and winced as a second shot blasted towards the glittering figure of Brett. It struck, expanding in a glow of fierce heat as the irillium cloak reflected its energy and sent little flecks of broken atoms scintillating through the air.

The scar-faced man cursed and aimed his squat-barrelled weapon directly at the pale face before him. He grinned savagely as his finger tightened on the trigger, and deliberately took his time over the shot. It proved his death.

Something flashed from beneath the glittering cloak, something like a rapier of brilliant flame, hissing slightly as it disrupted the atoms of the air, and stabbing in a shaft of eye-searing brilliance towards the scar-faced man. It hit and the sound of its striking was as the crash of thunder. Abruptly the tongue of flame died, and something fell heavily to the floor.

A body, seared and blackened, a dulled pistol held in one limp hand and where the head should have been, a mass of charred and smoking ash.

Sickly, Kerron stumbled towards the door and the cool night air.

7

Dark revelation

Silence. Silence broken only by the soft purr of functioning machines and the thin high presence of the supersonic whine from the hyper-drive. Kerron rested wakeful in his narrow bunk, his eyes wide and staring at the smooth curve of the hull plates, his ears strained and tense as he sought to catch fresh sound quivering through the ship.

He thought of the swirling greyness of hyperspace, pressing around them with tenuous fingers of unknown menace. He thought of the coldly glittering stars, and he remembered the chill he always felt when he stared at their distant vastness. He thought of the swift and violent action in the ramshackle building on some unnamed world, and felt his stomach heave as he remembered the charred and seared thing that had once been a man.

He stirred a little, and a voice whispered from a bunk opposite.

'Kerron, are you awake?'

'Chang! I thought that you were asleep.'

'No.' The Eurasian lifted himself on one arm, and in the dim light Kerron could see thin lines of worry etched deep on the bland yellow features.

'I am worried, Kerron. Why did we stop and pick up a woman?'

'You know about that?' Kerron turned in his bunk and stared at the dimly lit face of his friend. Chang nodded.

'Yes. Forrest and I were awake when you returned. Who is she, Kerron?'

'I don't know, a piano player from some outpost town. Brett seemed to know her, and she knew him.' Kerron paused as he remembered how they had left the shanty. 'A man tried to kill Brett, a scar-faced man. Brett shot him and we returned to the ship. Some others tried to stop us and Brett shot them also. I don't know what it was all about, Brett didn't talk about it.'

'You know her name?'

'Nyeeda. A tall woman, no longer young but very beautiful.' He sighed a little as he remembered just how beautiful he had thought her. Chang bit his lips.

'Why are we here, Kerron?' he whispered. 'Lying here with the throb of the hyper-drive ringing through my head, I have been thinking about it, and the whole thing seems to make less and less sense. A man told us that with our help he could solve the secret of immortality, and because that man had lived for longer than any other man known, we believed him. We left Earth, left everything we owned, trusted him with our lives and all our hopes. Why? Why should we believe him?'

'I don't know,' Kerron said slowly. 'I hadn't really thought about it. I trust Brett as a child trusts an adult. There is no reason to it, I just feel that he is reliable.' He smiled a little as he stared at the dimly lit face of his friend

'What else can we do?'

'Nothing,' said Chang, 'and yet . . . ' He glanced over to where Forrest lay in uneasy slumber. 'Forrest has something up his sleeve, Kerron, something he hasn't told us. I have a suspicion of what it is, and we must be careful you and I.'

'How do you mean, Chang?'

'Forrest is a greedy man, a man consumed with a secret desire, and he will stop at nothing to achieve it.'

'What can he do?' Kerron stared at the restless figure in the narrow bunk. 'Out here we are equal with each other, and all of us are dependant on Brett.'

'Equal?' Chang shrugged. 'I could argue about that, but what of the mysterious ship waiting on the edge of Brett's radar screen?'

'That!' Kerron laughed and shook his head. 'How do I know what that was, Chang? It wasn't my ship, I know that, perhaps . . . ' He stared at the bland Eurasian. 'Forrest?'

'Who else?'

'Impossible! How would he communicate?'

'I don't know, but it would be interesting to discover whether or not that ship is still following us. If it is, then we must decide what we are to do.'

'You think that if we do discover the secret, Forrest may attempt to keep it for himself?'

'Yes.'

'I see.' Kerron sat silently biting his lips in thought. It was possible, too possible. He had no doubt as to Forrest's innate greed, and he knew what a temptation such a discovery would present to a man with an overwhelming ambition. With the secret of immortality a man could well become utter ruler of the universe. He glanced a little helplessly at Chang, 'What can we do?'

'I don't know, yet, but I would be happier if we had more information. We have taken far too much on trust.' With a smooth motion the Eurasian swung from his bunk. 'I suggest that we learn a little more from Brett himself. He is in the control room with that woman, perhaps if we listen to what they say . . . '

'Eavesdrop you mean?'

'Why not? We have too much to lose to be squeamish. Well?'

Slowly Kerron rose and joined the impatient figure of his companion.

Voices spilled from the control room. Soft voices, filtering past the half-open door, and sending faint echoes from the metal of walls and bulkheads. Tense, shivering a little in the chill of the corridor, Kerron and Chang crouched tensed against the cold metal, listening.

Glass clicked on metal and someone stirred with a dry rustle of clothing. Shadows flickered and someone sighed, the faint sound echoing thinly from the surrounding metal.

'How long has it been, Nyeeda?'

'Does it matter, Brett, now?' Her voice was low, yet rich and full of human warmth and emotion. Kerron glanced at Chang, almost invisible in the dim lighting, and nodded at the other's questioning whisper. She sighed again, and they could hear Brett stirring as he moved restlessly in his cushioned chair.

'We parted, you and I, Brett, and for me time ceased until your return. How long?' She laughed a little, a laugh without humour. 'Half a lifetime perhaps? A quarter? Do you remember?'

'No!' Brett sounded unnaturally harsh.

'I have lost track of time, all the arid years, the years of hope and dying faith. I remember you, how could I forget, but I had to wait for the right moment, it came, and we are together again.'

'For how long, Brett?' There was a peculiar note of strained urgency in her low tones. 'For how long?'

'I hope, forever.'

The listeners caught the sharp sound of her indrawn breath, the little catch of emotion in her throat, and for a moment Kerron caught the impression of unshed tears.

'Are you sure, Brett? Are you certain?'

'No.'

Kerron felt the breath of an icy chill as he heard the flat tones of the tall adventurer, and he shivered as the cold sweat of fear started on his quivering body. Chang gripped his arm until he almost screamed with the pain, then together they waited, listening.

'How can I be certain?' Brett spoke flatly, with a peculiar deadness to his tones, as a man might speak who has forgotten that others are listening. 'For how long have we hoped, and how many times have I been disappointed? I cannot be certain, but if the secret of immortality does not lie behind The Wall, then it does not exist in the whole wide galaxy, and I have lived in vain.'

'Don't say that, Brett!' Clothing rustled at sudden motion, and shadows thrown from the dim instrument lights flickered over the cold metal. 'You cannot say that! What if the secret does not exist, would it matter so much?'

'You say that, Nyeeda?' Brett laughed softly, yet with an aching bitterness that brought a sudden choking sensation to Kerron's throat. 'You of all people should know.'

'Yes, Brett. I know.'

Silence. Silence as each was busy with their own secret thoughts, and the thin high quiver of the supersonic sent little tremors racing over sensitive skin and jerked at tense nerves. The woman sighed, and footsteps rang hollowly as someone approached the door. Quickly Chang drew Kerron away from the control room, darting down the corridor and halting in the deep shadows leading to the engine room.

Light streamed from the fully-opened door, and for a moment two figures stood limned against the light. Then the smaller of the two, the woman, walked down the metal passageway and entered one of several empty compartments. Brett stood for a moment watching her, then at the click of a lock his shoulders slumped, and he seemed to be very tired.

Chang grunted softly, and before Kerron could stop him, had strode from the deep shadows and entered the control room. Kerron hesitated, then at the low murmur of voices shrugged and followed the Eurasian.

'So you were listening?' Brett leaned against the control panel, his figure a glitter of light from the twinkling spots on the instrument dials, and stared coldly at them from the deathly whiteness of his hard features.

'Yes.' Chang stared directly at the tall adventurer, then deliberately sat down on the padded control chair. 'We heard a little, enough to know that you are taking us on a wild chase, taking us for your own reasons, and I want to know more.'

'Isn't it a little late for that?' Brett smiled and sat down, gesturing for Kerron to join them. 'I haven't lied to you. I still hope that beyond The Wall we will all find what we most want, but how can I be certain?'

'So it is a gamble.' Kerron sat tiredly in the soft chair.

'Yes, but a gamble in which the odds are on our side.' Brett paused, staring at the swirling grey mist writhing against the visi-screen. 'I cannot be certain, who can? If science can find the answer to the unknown, then science points to beyond The Wall. There we shall find the secret of creation and with that secret we shall have solved all lesser ones, including the secret of eternal life. I am sure of this.'

He smiled at them, his grey eyes suddenly warm and human against the cold whiteness of his face. 'I need you, in that I did not lie. You are the ones who will force this ship past The Wall. You, with your desperate longing for life, you will struggle on where other men would yield, for you have the one great incentive.'

'We have?' Chang pursed his lips. 'What is that?'

'You are dying men, all of you. Either you do as I order, or die, and I will not be the one to cause your death.' Brett stirred as he glanced at the banked instruments.

'I lied to you in one thing, you will not live a year, but you will live long enough to do what has to be done.' He moved with a ripple of reflected light as he adjusted one of the rheostats on the control panel, then turned to face them.

'This means as much to me as it does to you,' he said quietly. 'Perhaps more.'

'How can it?' Kerron sat quivering with an inner dread his face and neck moist with a chilly sweat. 'You have everything we need, you already have immortality, how can you know the terrible fear which drives other men. To you this is just an expedition, if you fail, then you can always try again, but us . . . ' He sat staring sickly at the coiling grey mist of hyperspace. 'We can never try again.'

'You think that?' Brett smiled and then sighed as he stared past them into the dim vistas of the past. 'I have lived a long time,' he murmured. 'Too long I have watched the swift and sudden growth of a wondrous flower, first a thin green shoot, rising to sturdy strength bright with hope and fed with the ambitions of many men, and that was the conquest of space. I have seen that bright strong shoot break into sudden flower, seen the unfolding petals of abrupt expansion as men swept from their confines and headed towards the stars, and that was the invention of the hyper-drive which gave the galaxy to the race of Man. I have watched that flower wilt and die, and in its place have seen the succulent fruits of final success, and that was when man and alien could meet and each call the other brother. All this I have seen, and I am tired. Tired of walking alone to be forever debarred from the normal comforts of men. Tired of being watched and envied and hated by men who age and die, die cursing me for having what they believe they want most of all.'

'Isn't that natural?' murmured Chang. 'Can you blame them?'

'Would you like to be what I am?' Brett stared at the calm yellow features of the Eurasian with sudden challenge. 'Would you exchange the life you have had for the life I must lead?'

'Yes.'

'It is easy to say that,' murmured the tall adventurer, 'but do you know what you ask? I do not wear irillium because I like it, spun metal is not the best material for garments, the weight alone is sometimes more than I can carry. I wear it because it is the one metal which is opaque to radiation.' He smiled at the sudden gleam of understanding in the yellow man's eyes.

'Yes. Radiation! I told you that I was exposed to a burst of tremendously hard radiant energy, it did not leave me unaffected.' He paused, staring again at the glittering bank of instruments. 'Each time I take a bath I must be careful how I dispose of the waste water, it is radioactively 'hot'. I can never nurse a pet, I would kill it, and for the same reason I can never join normal men in their normal pursuits.' He smiled at

Chang. 'Now do you begin to understand?'

Slowly the Eurasian nodded. 'No children, of course, and no wife, no . . . ' He looked compassionately at the tall adventurer.

'Exactly. I can never know the warmth of a woman's arms, never know a woman's kiss, the sweet forgetfulness of natural love. I must be always alone, always! Can you realise what that can mean?'

'No children,' murmured the Eurasian. 'If I were to believe in the religion of my ancestors, that would be tragedy enough, and even in this modern age I can realise what it could mean.'

'Loneliness, utter and complete loneliness. To be almost immortal, and yet to have to walk alone through the dragging years. To see other men enjoying the things I would willingly die to obtain, and to see the envy in their eyes as they stare at me.' Brett laughed curtly and without humour.

'Then the woman, Nyeeda?' Kerron glanced uneasily at the control room door.

'A friend.' Brett stared again at the banked instruments.

'Are we taking her with us?'

'Yes.'

'Is it wise?' Chang folded his arms and smiled his bland smile. Brett shrugged.

Abruptly alarms rang throughout the ship, and the control panel blazed with light.

8

Into the rift

Smoothly, Brett swung in his padded chair and faced the flashing control panel. Deftly he adjusted rheostats and closed circuits, the lights died and the shrill clangour of the alarms faded into silence.

'Take your positions!' he snapped. 'We're breaking out of hyperspace.'

'Now!' Chang stared at the swirling mist coiling against the visi-screen. 'Are we there?'

'Get to your engines, Chang! Kerron! Get into the other chair. Hurry!' Tensely, Brett bent over the controls and carefully adjusted the knurled verniers of several controls. He paused, his hand resting on a short lever.

'Ready?'

Kerron nodded, swallowing against the fear clogging his throat. Emergence from hyperspace always had its dangers. They

115

could break back into the normal universe too near a sun, too near a planet, or even within a body of matter itself. Such emergence would mean sudden and violent death as two objects strove to occupy the same space at the same time. Matter would blend with matter, for the merest fraction of time titanic forces would strive and strain the very fabric of the space-time continuum itself as they fought to maintain the balance of natural law, they would fail, and the ship would volatize into incandescent vapour, the ship and all it contained.

'Ready?' repeated Brett. He glanced sharply at Kerron. 'Is anything wrong? Are you ill?'

'No.' Kerron forced himself to smile. 'Ready.'

'Then here we go.' Deliberately Brett pressed the lever, and from the engine room came a shrilling whine as tremendous power surged and flowed through the frost-covered coils of the humped hyper-drive engines.

Strain gripped them. Strain, and the nerve quivering throb of dampened supersonic vibrations. Kerron swallowed repeatedly as he strove to master his fear. His stomach churned as alien strains gripped him, twisting and forcing his body into unnatural patterns, blurring his vision, and making his heart thud against his ribs.

The tension grew, and for one horrible moment Kerron thought that he was being turned inside out, then it was over and weakly he stared at the glittering panorama of outer space.

'Better now?' Brett stared at the visi-screen as his hands darted over the controls. From the gaping venturis at the stern of the vessel long fingers of blue-white flame stabbed towards the distant stars, and the ship trembled to the thrust of the mighty engines.

'Yes.' Kerron wiped his streaming face and neck. 'Are we there?'

'Almost.' Brett stared at the glittering screen. 'Something peculiar is happening. A ship has just broken out of hyperspace, the same ship which has been following us since we left Earth.' He looked coldly at Kerron. 'Is it yours?'

'No.'

'Then it must belong to either Chang or Forrest. I wouldn't be surprised to find it was Forrest's.' He laughed scornfully. 'The fool! Does he think that it can follow us to where we're going?'

'Where is that?' Kerron ignored the other's question as he stared at the star-shot night of space. Brett pointed to where a dark patch half-covered the visi-screen.

'There! See it? That dark smear against the stars, looks like a great cloud of dust particles, but it isn't.'

'What is it then?'

'The rift, an opening, in The Wall. We are going through it.'

'Now?'

'Now!' Deliberately Brett depressed the firing lever of the main rocket drive and the ship trembled to the thrust of high acceleration.

Chang came from the engine room, his yellow face glistening with sweat, and close behind Forrest stumbled, his thin features twisted with pain as he clutched at his chest. Brett glanced at him, and wordlessly shook three green tablets from a phial.

'Take these.' The tall adventurer glanced at the other two. 'Do either of you feel pain?'

'No.'

'Do you, Chang?'

'No, should I?'

'Not yet.' Brett stared at them, then at Forrest. 'If any of you feels any sort of discomfort at all, heart pain, nervous irritation, anything, let me know at once. We are heading for the rift, and all of you must be at the peak of efficiency.'

'The Wall!' Forrest stepped forward peering at the visi-screen, he glanced once at the dark patch before them then let his eyes drift over surrounding space. Brett watched him with a faint smile.

'Looking for something, Forrest? A ship perhaps?'

'No,' muttered the bald man, 'just curious.'

A click from the door warned them of the entrance of the remaining member of the party, and silently they watched as the woman joined them in the control room.

She seemed tired, with heavy lines marring the smooth perfection of her beauty, and her large, slightly slanted eyes burned in the whiteness of her face. Her thick black hair was loose, falling in long rippling coils to her shoulders, and for a moment Kerron thought that he stared at a young girl. She moved, and with the motion came reality.

'Nyeeda!' Brett stepped forward, and again Kerron had the impression of inner strain as the tall adventurer forced himself to remember not to take her in his arms.

'I heard the alarms,' she said heavily. 'Is anything wrong?'

'No, nothing wrong.' Brett moved so that he stood beside her, and his cold grey eyes held a world of tender passion as he stared down at her pale upturned face. 'We have arrived.'

'The Wall?'

'Yes.'

'I see.' She sighed and slumped down into one of the padded chairs. 'This is the end then?'

'No!' Brett moved with a quick ripple of flashing colour. 'Not the end, the beginning! We are at the threshold of a great new adventure, and soon we should know the very last secret of life!' He breathed heavily as he stared at the growing dark splotch on the visi-screen. 'Beyond The Wall lies the secret of creation, the very birthplace of life! I am certain of it, and we will be the first to discover the real truth of the universe!'

'Brave words,' sneered Forrest, 'to be expected from a man like you, but what guarantee have we that all this isn't a mad delusion from an insane mind?'

'None.' Brett was very calm, but the expression of his eyes made Kerron glad that it was not he who had spoken.

'Rave as you will,' continued Forrest, 'I am not impressed, but there is a thing we must decide.'

'Yes?'

'What of the woman?'

'Nyeeda? What of her?'

'Why is she here?' Forrest glanced at the others. 'We paid for your services, paid highly, and we did not pay for passengers to be carried at our expense.'

'Speak for yourself,' snapped Kerron

sharply. 'I do not object to the woman.'

'Nor I,' echoed Chang.

'I do!' Forrest glared at the silent figure slumped into the padded chair. 'Who is she? Why are we carrying her? Where are we going? I think that you had better answer me, Brett!'

For a moment Kerron thought that the tall adventurer would smash his gloved hand into the sneering face of Forrest. He tensed, little ripples of colour betraying the slight motion of his muscles, then the woman touched him on the arm and he relaxed.

'It is a long story,' he said quietly, 'and I must appeal to your charity if for nothing else. Nyeeda is a mutant, a person whose blood contains some subtle difference, which makes it impossible for her to enter the vaults on Calistrana, to wait for the solving of the secret of immortality in suspended animation. She will die, and nothing any man can do can save her, like yourselves she has but one hope, and that hope lies beyond The Wall.'

'What is she to you?' Forrest stared at the silent woman with burning eyes. 'A mutant! A semi-human thing!'

'I love her.' Brett didn't raise his voice he didn't even move from where he stood, but light glimmered with sudden flashes from the irillium of his garments, and the pitted orifice of a weapon stared at the shrinking figure of the bald-headed man. 'Say no more, Forrest, say no more. I will burn you to ash if you say another word!'

'Brett!' The woman stirred in the chair and clutched at the adventurer's arm. 'Brett!'

'No, Nyeeda, leave me alone. There are some things no man can stand, and you are my weakness.' He stared at the others, his grey eyes as cold and as hard as the glittering stars reflected on the visi-screen. 'I love her, do you understand? I have loved her from the first moment we met, and my life since then has been a battle with time. Time to defeat the inevitable march of approaching death. I would save her if I could, but the little I have to offer is useless, and the sands of her life are running out. If immortality lies beyond The Wall, she will share it, she will share it though none other in the whole galaxy may ever learn the secret again. If life for her lies on the other side of The Wall, then it is hers, hers above all else.'

He staggered a little as the ship gave a sudden lurch, and abruptly the control panel blazed with warning lights. Deftly he holstered the weapon and with a lithe movement slipped into the pilot's chair. Tersely he snapped quick orders.

'Chang, to your engines. Forrest, go with him. Kerron, join me here. Nyeeda, to your cabin and wait.'

The ship lurched again, and the scream of surging power shrilled from the engine room. Chang grabbed Forrest and raced down the corridor, the sounds of their footsteps lost among the whining of tormented machinery. Nyeeda hesitated, then as Kerron strapped himself into the co-pilot's chair; shrugged and left the control room. Tensely Brett leaned over the control panel.

With quick motions of his hands he stopped the lurching of the vessel, fed power into the main drive and increased the speed of the stabilising gyroscopes. Weight dragged at them, mounting with the pulsing thunder of the rockets, and Kerron winced as his ears ached with the shrilling vibration from the metal of the hull plates and bulkheads.

'Kerron, watch that target star, watch what I do.' Brett spoke with the corner of his mouth, his eyes never leaving the shifting pattern of stars on the visi-screen.

'We are at the outermost eddy currents of the rift, a surging cross-tide of electronic forces. It is essential to steer the ship by manual control, we can't trust the automatics. I have taken a star sight, your job will be to keep the crosshairs centred on the target star.' He pointed with a swift motion of one hand.

'See it? I've adjusted the rear visi-screen, there's nothing directly before us by which to steer. Just keep that star centred, now watch and learn the controls from my actions.'

Deftly his hands darted over the controls, feeding power to opposed steering-tubes, stabbing at the void with brilliant tongues of blue-white fire, ions emitted by the atomic pile in the engine room, focused by magnetic currents, and shot from the gaping venturis at almost the speed of light.

They streamed from the rocket tubes, thrusting the ship with a direct mass-speed ratio, so that even though their mass was small, yet their tremendous velocity and their infinite number sent the ship veering on its course. Like a ship tossing in some invisible current the vessel plunged through space, and always the miles-long streamers of brilliant flame from the main drive thrust them onwards, onwards towards the growing patch of utter darkness before them.

Time passed, long weary hours of continual acceleration pressure, of stomach-twisting manoeuvres, of the ear-paining shrill of metallic vibration from the quivering hull plates. Still, the ship jerked beneath the impact of strange forces, and still Brett sat, his hands flickering over the controls as he guided the ship through the surging electronic storm.

Kerron sat numb with fear and pain, little trickles of blood running from his ears and nose, mingling with sweat and burning as it touched his tender skin. Once he felt as though his throbbing head would split with sheer agony, and once he almost screamed with pain as a cold hand seemed to squeeze his heart, but grimly he fought to retain consciousness and his burning eyes followed every move of the pilot's darting hands.

Suddenly it was over.

Suddenly the ship seemed free of the terrible opposing forces, the lurching stopped, the veering, the muscle-wrenching strain. Thankfully, Kerron slumped back in his chair as he watched Brett release the main drive controls, and breathed gratefully at the lifting of the savage acceleration pressure.

'Are we there?'

'What!' Brett laughed as he rose from the chair and stretched with a ripple of brilliant colour. 'That was the easy part, I have done it often.' He stared seriously down at Kerron.

'We have passed the outer eddy-currents, that is all, the hard part is yet to come. We will rest for a while, check the ship for damage, arrange watches, and then make the final effort.'

'Will it take long, the final penetration I mean?'

'I don't know, I have never wholly managed to get right through.' Brett stared at the control panel and made a slight adjustment. 'Always before I have had to turn back, either my crew mutinied, or as on the last time, I had to rest and the automatics failed me. The ship spun, was twisted by the blast of radiant energy from The Wall, and when I awoke I was too far to return.' He shook his head. 'We have a breathing space, no more, and it is the last we will have for a long time.'

'What is it?' Kerron stared at the great splotch of blackness before them, occupying almost all of the surface of the visi-screen. 'Why can't we just blast straight through?'

'For the same reason that a ship, a sea going vessel I mean, has trouble advancing against a strong current of water. We are opposed by a streaming surge of radiation, energy, electronic flow, call it what you will. It thrusts us back, forces us to use every trick of navigation we know. It takes power to oppose it, tremendous power, this ship has five times the rocket drive necessary for a vessel of its class, and still we may not get through.'

'I can understand that, but why the lurching?'

'Think of us as a rowboat going up a river against a strong current,' explained Brett. 'While the rower can keep the bow of the boat directly in line with the current, the resistance is lowered and he can make progress. If the boat should veer, turn sidewise to the current, then it would be forced downstream, and unless the rower could straighten it, he would lose all headway.' He glanced at the visa-screen and pointed towards the rear-view plate.

'We must steer by that target-star, while it is in line with our axis. We are on the right course, as soon as we lose that course, then we are being thrown back away from The Wall.'

'I see,' Kerron said slowly, 'but how far have we to go, and following your analogy, won't the radiant pressure increase the nearer we get to the rift?'

Brett shrugged. 'Maybe, and then again, maybe not. This is space remember, and we know little of conditions in this particular sector. I am hoping that we can pass the full force of the electronic currents and find a second area of calm. We must wait and see.'

Noise suddenly echoed from the outer corridor. The sound of shouting and the footsteps of two men. Chang cried out in a loud voice, and was answered by a horrible whimpering. The control room door burst open and something half-fell into the room.

Kerron stared and felt cold fear grip his heart. It was Forrest, and he was *old*!

9

Journey into hell

He lay on the metal flooring, his hairless scalp glistening in the glow from the tube-lights, and his seamed and lined features were twisted with anger and fear.

'Kerron,' he gasped. 'Chang! Help me!'

'I noticed him a few moments ago,' wheezed the yellow-skinned Eurasian. He wiped sweat and blood from his face and neck. 'I was tending the engines, and when I looked around I saw him.' He shuddered a little at the memory. 'I tried to get him here without his knowing, but he saw his reflection on a bulkhead, and for a while he almost went crazy.'

'What is it?' Kerron stared wildly at the tall adventurer. 'Brett! Why is he so old?'

A ripple of colour and a flashing of reflected light limned the room as the tall man knelt beside the whining thing on the metal floor. Gently he raised each eyelid, touched the great vein of the throat, and then slowly rose to his feet.

'Carry him to his bunk,' he said tiredly. 'I will attend him, but there is little I can do.'

'Can't you revive him?' Kerron forced himself to remain calm. 'You did it once, can't you do it again?'

'No.'

Gently Kerron and Chang carried Forrest to his bunk, Brett following. Nyeeda peered from her half-open door, hesitated for a moment, then followed them into the room. Brett smiled at her, and nodded towards Forrest.

'A job for you, Nyeeda. He must be nursed, will you do it?'

'Of course.' Fire gleamed deep in her dark eyes as she stared at the whimpering man. 'I shall take great care of him, Brett, you can trust me for that.'

'Good.' Abruptly the tall adventurer swung into rapid motion. He opened a compact medical kit, loaded several hypodermics with a scintillating blue fluid, and slid the needles beneath the wrinkled skin of the man on the bunk. He watched as Forrest calmed, began to breathe easier, and had lost his first half-insane expression. Brett smiled down at the man, and adjusted the equipment for the continuous transfusion of blood plasma.

'The main cause of his breakdown was fear,' he said in a detached voice. 'Extreme fear. It upset his glandular balance and allowed the rapid catabolism of his body cells. Normally it wouldn't have mattered, a normal man can adjust to such extremes, but he was not normal, and neither are you.' He looked fixedly at Kerron and Chang.

'This may happen to either of you, happen at anytime, and there is nothing I can do to stop it. You must force yourselves to remain calm, not to get too excited, to avoid all intense emotion. Remember that you are living an unnatural life, an artificial life where the limits of tolerance are not very wide. If you should happen to go over the edge, then you will be as he is.' He stared down at the man on the bunk.

'Will he die?' whispered Chang.

'Not yet, he has used almost all of his artificially induced vitality, but not all. He will live with care and with what little help I can give him.' Carefully Brett slid a thick needle into the great vein of the arm, and adjusted the flow of plasma.

'I am going to replace his blood with fresh plasma, it has been strengthened with anti-bodies and irradiated with helpful radiation. With plentiful doses of energen prophylactic drugs and a trickle electronic life charge, he will recover a little, but he will never be the same as he once was.'

'Who will watch over him?' Chang stared at the silent figure of the woman barely concealing his distrust.

'Nyeeda.'

'Couldn't one of us do it?'

'No. I need you at the engines, Chang, and Kerron must relieve me at the control panel.' He glanced at the Eurasian in sudden understanding. 'Don't you trust her?'

'Forrest didn't like her,' evaded Chang. 'She may not like him.'

'Nyeeda is a born nurse.' Brett smiled

as he looked at her. 'I know. Remember she is a mutant, an unsuccessful one, and because of that a tormented woman. She has a tremendously high maternal instinct, but she can never bear children. Her frustrated instincts take the form of a selfless desire to help others, she will make a good nurse for Forrest.' Brett took the woman by the shoulders and swung her to face him. He dropped his hands from her, and something warm and terribly human shone in the cold depths of his grey eyes.

'Take care of him, Nyeeda,' he whispered. 'Take good care.'

She nodded, and sat down beside the plastic and metal of the plasma equipment, watching the steady flow with unblinking eyes.

Silence fell, unbroken aside from the little normal sounds present in any living ship, the gentle pulse of hidden currents of power, the slight hiss from the air-conditioners, and the muted sounds of men snatching uneasy sleep.

Kerron started, his heart thudding against his ribs, and stared upwards at the pale face of Brett.

'Ready, Kerron?' The tall adventurer smiled as he waited for the white-haired man to climb from his bunk. Chang had already awoken and stood waiting by the narrow doorway. Kerron nodded, and wiped his tired eyes.

'Are we there?'

'Almost.' Brett led the way to the control room and pointed at the visi-screen. The dark patch now covered the plate, sprawling before them like an immense splotch of menacing nothing-ness. Kerron stared at it, and felt the sudden return of an age-old fear. He licked dry lips and tried to smile.

'How long?'

'Soon now.' Brett lifted a loaded hypodermic and wordlessly injected the contents into Kerron's arm. He repeated the action with Chang, and replaced the instrument in a wall cabinet.

'From now until we penetrate The Wall, we can expect no rest, it will be continuous effort all the way and without the proper mental adjustment you would never live through it. One thing you must remember, you get through — or die! There will be no second chance, no time for another attempt. You haven't long to live, and unless we manage to penetrate the first time, then you will never penetrate at all.'

'You don't have to keep telling us that,' snarled Kerron. 'We know.'

'Then don't forget it!' Brett sighed and rubbed at his eyes. 'That injection I gave you will help a little against space hallucinations. If you feel that you just can't carry on a moment longer, take one of these green tablets, but don't take too many of them. I shall alternate between the engines and the control panel, but you must both do your share.'

He glanced at the array of glittering instruments on the control panel. 'It will be very soon now. Get to your stations!'

Hastily Kerron strapped himself in the co-pilot's chair, and dimly heard Chang's running footsteps as he headed for the engine room. Brett stabbed at a button and spoke into the intercom.

'Control to engine room. Ready?'

'Engine to control. Ready!'

'Good. Feed maximum power at all times. Keep ozone content of air below index three, and electrostatic charge below index nine.'

'Received and understood.'

'Right.'

Brett opened the circuit and gently depressed the firing levers of the main rocket drive. From the stern of the vessel a low thundering grew and grew and grew into a vibrating roar of unleashed power. Sound, transmitted from the gaping venturis along the metal of the hull and internal structure of the vessel, quivered and throbbed all around. It rang from metal, pulsed through the circulating air, set up resonances in flesh and bone and brain. It snarled, and shrilled from every atom of the ship, yelling a song of tremendous power and beneath the savage drive of that power, the ship plunged forward.

Acceleration pressure clamped down on them, weight piled on chests and stomachs, coated arms and necks with lead, pressed down on skulls and made the very air almost solid and hurtful to breathe. Needles quivered and swung on jewelled bearings, climbing upwards along the graduated faces of the dials, telling of the exhaust velocity, the temperature, the mass content of expelled fuel ions blasted away from the raging inferno of the firing chambers of the great rocket tubes.

Kerron whimpered, then bit his lip until he tasted the warm saltiness of blood, gripping the arms of his padded chair until his muscles ached and burned with useless effort. Deliberately he forced himself to relax, to cease the useless struggle against acceleration pressure, to yield rather than resist. Before him, the target-star seemed to wink and sneer, a cold and distant furnace blazing in the cold blackness of outer space, and yet far preferable to the swelling menace of the blackness before them.

Brett smiled a little without humour, and pressed still harder on the firing lever. From somewhere behind them a woman screamed, screamed and fell abruptly silent. The song of the rocket dive rose, became a thing of shrilling menace pounding at nerves and sinews, sending little ripples of sheer agony lancing along each fibre and cell.

Abruptly the ship lurched!

'This is it!' Brett smiled with a flash of white teeth, and gripped the steering levers until the knuckles showed through the thin fabric of his gloves. 'Hold on!'

Grimly, Kerron forced himself to prepare for battle.

It was hell! It was a blur of continual effort, a muscle wrenching agony of strain and watchful readiness. He relieved Brett, and shuddered to the lurching of the ship as the cross-currents of radiant energy tore and blasted against the metal of the ship. Grimly he fastened his eyes on the pale gleam of the target-star, and summoned every scrap of mental and physical strength to control the shuddering vessel. Dimly he realised that their speed had slowed, that even though the great rocket tubes still spewed their stabbing tongues of blue-white fire, yet something was slowing them down.

Time passed, dragging on leaden feet, each second weighted and horrible with pain. He relieved Brett, then rested for a while as the tall adventurer took his place at the controls. He relieved Brett, then was relieved, then took his place again. On and on, without rest, without any hint that the ordeal must soon be over, and still alien storms lashed at them, and the shrilling from the overdriven rocket tubes scratched at the surface of his quivering brain.

His vision began to blur, to fill the ship with a coiling grey mist, a mist from which strange faces peered and grimaced, grinning and nodding as they licked pendulous lips and stared with horrible eyes. Tiredly he recalled the old space-men's legends, the tall tales told by the first explorers of the void. Radiation was flooding the vessel, disturbing the delicate neuron paths of his brain, causing hallucinations and delirium.

Knowing the cause did not help dispel the illusions, and weakly he swallowed three of the green tablets. Vitality flooded back into his weakened frame. Energy seemed to rush along his veins and with the new sense of well-being, his vision cleared and the grimacing faces vanished.

They would return he knew. No power known to man could shield a brain against hard radiation, not when that radiation poured and gushed from a region of space unknown to man, gushed in tremendous torrents of energy sufficient to slow even the hard driven ionic rockets of an overpowered ship.

He wiped his streaming features and stared a little stupidly at his bloodstained hand. He giggled, for some reason the sight was amusing, then sanity returned and he swallowed more green tablets, heedless of the pain around his heart.

Brett staggered into the control room, his pale face a mask of sweat and blood.

'We're not going to make it,' he gasped. 'Our progress is too slow, you'd never last out: and I can't do it alone.'

'What shall we do?' Kerron tried not to show his joy at the prospect of escape from the lunging hell that was the ship.

'I'm going to try something new. I've connected the hyper-drive on automatic circuit. We'll take short quick hops, realigning the ship each time we come out of hyperspace. It is the only way, if we don't do it, we might as well go home.'

Grimly he dropped into the pilot's chair and reached for the controls. A lever slid beneath his gloved hand and suddenly the ship twisted to the surge of tremendous forces. Kerron screamed, then sat shivering as he stared at the swirling grey mist of hyperspace. From somewhere a long way off he heard a man slowly begin to count.

'Three! Four! Five!'

Strain snatched at them. Terrible wrenching strain, and then Brett was jerking at the controls, fighting the dim point of the target-star back on to the crosshairs of the visi-screen.

Again strain gripped them, again the grey mist of hyperspace pressed coilingly against the plate of the featureless visi-screen. Again Brett counted slowly to five.

'No!' Kerron screamed and tried to rise from his chair. 'No!'

'Shut up!' Brett winced as they jerked from hyperspace and with desperate speed realigned the twisting vessel. 'It's the only way. Five seconds in, and five seconds out. Unless we do it, we'll all have lived in vain!'

Kerron shuddered, feeling a growing sickness at the pit of his stomach as the ship trembled beneath the space-tearing strain of a rapidly alternating hyper-drive field.

Power surged into the frost-covered coils of the engine, space warped and tore as the field was established, dropping with all it enclosed into some alien region where the normal laws of space and time did not apply. For five seconds they plunged through that strange region, then the power was drained from the field, drained back into the great accumulators, with a dimensional twisting of every atom the ship emerged into the hell of the electronic storm.

Five seconds each way. Five seconds of savage alternation while the insulation in the engine room smoked and stank, the accumulator plates warped and buckled, and the resonance of the shrilling metal grew into a destructive ultrasonic frequency.

It was more than normal men could bear!

The door of the control room burst open, and Chang stood coughing and gasping, his yellow face stained with soot and ugly wheals showing on his naked torso.

'The engines!' He swayed a little and fought for breath. 'The engines are burning out, the backlash of power has burned the insulation. Brett, we've got to stop!'

He staggered as the door slammed into him, and suddenly Nyeeda stood within the room.

Kerron stared at her with a sudden sickness churning at his stomach. The mutant was almost insane! She swayed a little, her eyes blazing in the whiteness of her features, and little sounds trickled from her parted lips. Even at her worst she was still beautiful, even now when her thick dark hair hung in wild disorder, and her smooth skin was marred with dirt and blood. She placed her hands to the side of her head, covering her ears, and screamed, and screamed, and kept on screaming. Watching her, Kerron suddenly understood.

'Space hallucinations,' he yelled at Brett. 'Give her an anti-radiation shot.'

'I can't.' Brett stared at the woman with hell in his eyes. 'Her blood is too different, it would kill her.'

Abruptly he rose with a ripple of coloured light and stepped before the shrieking woman. His hand clenched and moved in a short arc, the sound of the impact lost in the shrilling of the metal. Tenderly he caught her, and carried her to one of the chairs, strapping her against the soft cushions, and Kerron could see agony on his face.

Suddenly things grew blurred, pain gripped his heart, and the soft velvet blackness of oblivion swept over him.

10

Birthplace of Creation

Kerron sighed and moved a little, stretching his arms, and legs, seeming to float on a bank of soft white cloud and relaxing in utter contentment. Slowly he opened his eyes and stared for a long moment at the curved metal of the hull, frowning in bewilderment as he struggled to regain his memory. It came with a rush, and with a gasp of fear he sat up on something soft and yielding.

He was still strapped in one of the control chairs, the pneumatic cushions curving to fit every movement of his body. It was very quiet, the shrill of the thundering rockets had stopped, the screaming of surging power had died away, and all he could hear was the soft breathing of someone in the chair beside him.

It was Nyeeda. She rested quietly, her lips barely parted and a single coil of dark hair writhing over the pale perfection of her skin. She seemed very young, sleep and relaxation had smoothed the lines from her features, and looking at her, Kerron could understand how Brett must have felt about her when first they had met.

He moved, surprised at his own. weakness, and reached out a hand to catch at the edge of the control panel. He gripped, strained to raise himself, and suddenly stopped, staring at his hand.

It was a claw! A thin, shrivelled thing of bone and stringy muscle. The skin was cracked and tight-drawn over the hooked fingers, looking yellow and sere in the soft light streaming from the concealed lighting. With a gasp of horror he pulled himself from the chair and peered at the polished surface of a bulkhead.

His scream echoed throughout the ship, making Nyeeda stir in her sleep, and bringing Brett running on pounding feet.

'No!' Kerron staggered away from the bulkhead, and clawed desperately at his features.

'No.'

'Steady.' Brett supported him with one

metal-covered arm and reseated him in the control chair. 'Don't excite yourself, it's all over now.'

'All over?'

'Yes, we broke through, we're beyond The Wall!'

'Are we?' Kerron laughed hysterically and gestured with one claw-like hand. 'What of me? What happened to me, my face . . . !' He shuddered.

'I warned you what would happen.' Brett stared sympathetically down at the trembling figure of Kerron. 'You have grown old. It happened to Forrest, to Chang, and it happened to you.'

'Has Chang altered too?'

'Yes. Forrest has changed least of all, he rested all through the trip, unconscious most of the time and with a continuous flow of fresh blood passing through his body.' Brett moved with a sudden ripple of flashing colour. He stared at the visi-screen, his cold grey eyes glistening with emotion.

'We made it Kerron! Do you understand? We made it! We're at the birthplace of creation!'

'Are we?' Kerron stirred restlessly in his chair mourning his lost youth. He stared at the screen with rheumy eyes, feeling the tightening of his stomach muscles as he stared at the unfamiliar stars.

They blazed like tremendous jewels against the blackness of space. Red and green, yellow and flaming blue, white and orange. He stared at a glowing ball of pure gold, and gestured with his claw-like hand.

'The stars, they are coloured, why is that?'

'I don't know.' Brett stared at the screen, his pale face tense and thoughtful. 'I have taken star-sights, measured magnitude and relative distance. That golden one is at the very centre of this region of space. We are heading for it now.'

'Heading for it?' Kerron frowned with the querulousness of the very old, 'Without power?'

'Yes, the rocket tubes were damaged when we broke through, they fired while in hyperspace and the backlash of ionic energy fused the venturis, but we are moving by our own momentum.' He smiled a little as he gripped the edge of the control panel. 'You should have known that by the lack of gravity.'

Kerron nodded, and wrinkled his brows as he tried to think of something, something terribly important. He stared at the distant point of golden light, and wondered why the stars should be all of different colours. Memory came with a sudden rush, and he lunged half out of the chair as he strained his weak muscles against a non-existent gravity.

'The secret,' he gasped hoarsely, 'have you found it?'

'No.' Brett tightened his lips as he stared at the old man. 'How could I? We have just broken through, and I haven't even repaired the tubes, but I know where it is to be found.'

'Where?'

'At the centre, at the very birthplace of creation, the fountain of all life!'

'The golden sun?'

'Where else?' The tall adventurer stooped and lifted Kerron as though he were a thing of paper and paste. 'I must treat you, try and restore some of your vitality, there is work to be done, and you must do it.' Gently he carried the old man to his bunk.

Chang lay sleeping on one of the narrow cots, Forrest grimaced over the edge of another, his eyes hot and burning in the wrinkled whiteness of his seamed and lined features. He cackled as Brett rapidly injected Kerron with a scintillating blue fluid and arranged the plasma apparatus, and stared avidly at the broken wreck of what had once been a youthful body.

'So it got you too, eh Kerron?' He sniggered and shifted on his bunk. 'How much longer do you think you've got to live now?'

'Shut up, Forrest.' Chang moved carefully as he glared at the sniggering old man, the tubes of the plasma apparatus buried in one arm. 'Remember that you are older than we are, and in all probability will die first.'

He smiled at Brett. 'How much longer now?'

'I don't know.' Rapidly the tall

adventurer adjusted the plasma flow, then stepped back from the narrow bunk. 'I'll have to go outside and clear the main jets.' He frowned. 'There's something peculiar about this space. From outside observations The Wall appeared to enclose an area of more than a hundred light years in diameter, but my internal measurements show it to be not more than ten, a few hours on hyperdrive.'

'Why is that?' Chang stared interestedly at the light-limned adventurer, his drawn yellow features glistening in the soft light.

'It could be that The Wall is far thicker than we first thought or it could be something entirely different.'

'Such as?'

'Space itself could be altered here. Light may travel at a different speed, the very space-time continuum may be different from what we know.' Brett shrugged and made a final adjustment to the snaking tubes of the plasma apparatus.

'Rest easy for a while, sleep if you can.' He smiled down at the trembling figure of Kerron. 'Don't take it too hard, after all you have been old before, this should be nothing new.'

Kerron tried to smile back, but failed as he felt the pain of wasted hope. It wasn't the same, it could never be the same again, not after having known what it was to be young once more, to feel the smooth ripple of muscle strain over a swelling chest, to feel the rushing surge of blood and vitality. He sighed and closed his eyes, not seeing the expression on Brett's face as he left the room, Forrest leaned over the edge of his cot.

'Kerron! Chang! Now's the time for us to decide what we are to do.'

'How do you mean?' Chang stared at the bald-headed man, his yellow face bland and expressionless.

'You heard what Brett said. We are at the centre of this space, at the birthplace of creation. He knows where the secret is to be found, the secret of immortality.' Forrest sucked in his breath with a hiss.

'Think of it! Think of what we could do with such a secret! Why we'd own the galaxy, the universe, all of the universes. We'd be Emperors over the mightiest

Empire ever dreamed of!'

'If there is a secret.' Kerron sighed as he felt the smooth flow of fresh blood washing through his wasted body. 'How can we be sure that it is to be found?'

'It's here alright.' Forrest sounded strangely confident. 'Brett has tried everywhere else it could be, and he wouldn't have brought the woman unless he was certain. What I want to know is, what are we going to do about it?'

'What can we do?' Chang sat up on his bunk, carefully moving the trailing tubes of the plasma apparatus.

'We can steal the secret, or rather take what is ours.' Forrest glared defiantly at them. 'We paid for this expedition didn't we? Then whatever is found belongs to us by right. We let Brett find the secret, then we take it, take it and use it as it should be used.'

'Perhaps Brett will have his own ideas?' Chang slowly shook his head. 'I admire your plan, Forrest, but I fail to see how it could work.'

'Then you'll come in with me?'

'Perhaps.' The Eurasian smiled blandly

as he stared at Kerron. 'It intrigues me, but even if we do find the secret, how do we get away with it?'

'I have a ship waiting for me, a fast armed vessel.' Forrest nodded at Kerron's startled expression. 'Yes, that strange ship was mine, and it has followed us all the way across the galaxy, it may even have followed us beyond The Wall. We can take the secret, dispose of Brett and the woman and escape to join my waiting vessel. Once on board, no one can stop us. No one!'

'I see.' Kerron frowned, then stared at Forrest in sudden doubt. 'I don't get it. How do you communicate with the ship?' Forrest sniggered and winked at Chang.

'Simple. I have a mutant telepath on board, an idiot who is in rapport with my neural flow. Naturally we can't exchange complicated messages, but I can tell them to either 'Come', 'Follow', or 'Wait'.' He chuckled again and grinned proudly at them. 'I've lived too long to be careless, and I never did trust Brett. Well? Are you with me?'

'What happens to us once we're aboard

your ship?' Kerron tried not to let the disgust he felt echo in his voice. 'I know you, Forrest, would you hesitate to get rid of us the same as you plan to get rid of Brett?'

'No. I need you, both of you, no one man can rule a universe alone.' Forrest stared at them his eyes hot and burning in his wrinkled face. 'Don't be fools! You are old men, dying, without hope. Why rely on a money-hungry adventurer? Brett admitted that he only used us to further his own plans, why should you hesitate?'

'I . . . ' Chang stopped, stared towards the opening door of the metal room, and made a quick gesture for silence.

Tensely the three old men watched the slowly opening door.

Nyeeda entered the room. She moved slowly, as if she were in great pain, and the deep pools of her eyes made great black splotches against the deathly whiteness of her features. Her thick dark hair hung around her shoulders and the hand with which she gripped the edge of the lintel showed her knuckles white and glistening through her delicate skin.

'Brett!' she gasped. 'Brett, in danger, great danger . . . ' Abruptly she slumped unconscious to the metal floor, her eyelids fluttering and her breath catching in her throat. Chang cursed and sat up on the bunk staring at the mutant woman.

'In danger!' Abruptly he jerked the tubes from his arm, and pressed a thumb over the bleeding wound. 'We must help him.'

'Why?' Forrest grinned like an evil monkey. 'Let him die, we would be better off without him.'

'Are you insane?' The Eurasian glared at the bald old man. 'Kill him if you like, but not now, not before he has led us to the secret. Kerron! Are you able to stand yet?'

Grimly Kerron slid the plasma tubes from his arms and swung thin legs over the edge of the cot. He was weak, terribly weak, but fear drove strength into quivering limbs and pounding heart. Brett must not die! Not until he had found the secret of immortality, and not even then. Brett must be saved, at whatever cost to any of them, the tall adventurer must be saved. The hope of mankind rested on him, and he must not die!

Staggering with weakness, Kerron forced himself to cross the room and stoop over the unconscious woman. Desperately he swung his hand, again, again, the sound of the slaps echoing in the metal room. Nyeeda stirred, raised a trembling hand to her red-stained cheek, and stared at him with wondering eyes.

'Why did you hit me?'

'What is the danger threatening Brett?' Impatiently he shook her, and half raised his hand. 'Where is Brett?'

She stared at him, her eyes growing wide and dark and filled with fear. She grabbed at his arm and pulled herself to her feet, then stood breathing with quick short breaths while blood ran unheeded from her bitten lips.

'He's out there, out among all the voices.' With sudden strength she pounded at her head, her face distorted with pain. 'I can hear them, strange voices, calling, calling always calling.'

'Where?'

'Outside. Out in space where Brett is working; I'm afraid. Afraid I tell you. Afraid!'

Chang shrugged as he looked at the trembling woman then stared at Kerron. 'Space hallucinations?'

'Maybe.' Kerron bit his lip thoughtfully as he stared at the woman. 'Let's go into the control room,' he suggested. 'We should be able to see Brett on the visi-screens, if anything threatens him we may be able to help.'

'What of her?'

'Leave her here, she can rest for a while.' Gently he led the quivering woman to a bunk. 'Sleep if you can,' he told her quietly. 'We are going to help Brett.'

She smiled at him as a terrified child smiles at a familiar face, a smile of trust and easy confidence. Long lashes fluttered over her eyelids, and within seconds she breathed in an easy natural sleep. Quietly they left the room.

Light streamed through the uncovered observation ports, red and green, pale blue and deep yellow, the light from the blazing multi-coloured stars of this strange space. Eagerly Kerron stared at them, his heart thudding painfully against his ribs as he felt the age-old fear and fascination of those distant suns. Before them, glowing like a great ball of purest gold, the strange star at the centre of this space beckoned with promise and eternal hope.

Chang tugged at his arm, and gestured towards the visi-screen controls.

'Can you see him?'

'I don't know yet.' Kerron fumbled with the unfamiliar controls, sending the power surging through the pick-up plates on the outer skin of the ship, scanning space in each direction. He snorted, and bent more closely to his work, adjusting verniers with hands that refused to obey and persisted in overshooting the delicate adjustments he tried to make.

Impatiently he gripped his wrist with his other hand, and sweated with the strain of forcing old and withered muscles to obey his mental commands. Something glittered in one corner of the plate, something metallic and lit with a tongue

161

of searing flame. Chang grunted, and desperately Kerron re-adjusted the visi-screen.

Brett hung at the end of a thin line, the metal and plastic of his space suit reflecting the light of the coloured stars, He held a cutting torch, and with it burnt away the twisted metal clogging the gaping mouths of the great venturis.

He was not alone!

Fire hung about him. Flashing shapes of scintillating energy, shifting and darting about the bulbous space suit and hovering like great polyhedrons about both ship and man. They blazed with inner light, radiating in a flashing riot of ever-changing, crystalline objects half a man's height in diameter, and swarming like a mass of bees.

'What are they?' Chang stared at Kerron, his yellow features sickly beneath the multi-hued light.

'I don't know.' Kerron stared at them, fascinated by the constant interplay of colours. 'They must be what Nyeeda was talking about, remember she said that she heard voices out there.' He frowned, then shook his head. 'Mutants are funny, for all we know she may be a telepath, able to pick up thought impressions from those crystals.'

'How can she?' Chang snorted his disgust. 'Surely you don't think that those things can be alive?'

'Maybe, maybe not. What is life? What is thought?' Kerron shrugged, and began to fumble in a locker. He dragged a mass of metal and fabric from the compartment, and straightening the space suit, began to wriggle into the suit. Weakness overpowered him, and he stared at the Eurasian.

'Help me will you, Chang?'

'What are you going to do?'

'I'm going out there to help Brett. I'll take a couple of guns, they may scare those things away from the ship, but we just can't sit in here and do nothing.'

Chang smiled and pointed at the instrument panel. Three dials had their needles pressed against the stops, high in the red, and seeing him, Kerron slumped in sudden despair.

11

The immortals

For hours it seemed they waited in the control room watching the solitary figure working on the clogged jets and tensely counting the increasing number of strange polyhedrons gathering about the ship. Twice Kerron attempted to don the space suit, and each time Chang pointed at the instrument panel with silent warning. The dials told more than words, and Kerron had to admit defeat.

No normal man could live outside the ship. The entire area of space was filled with a blasting mass of hard radiation, radiation so intense that a man would wither and die from radiant poisoning within minutes of leaving the insulated hull.

Impatiently they watched as the metallic figure on the screen finished his work, and Kerron sighed with relief as he heard the thud of the outer port. Seconds passed, long seconds as air rushed into the airlock, the pressure equalled, and slowly the inner port swung open.

'Wait!' Chang gripped his arm, and Kerron glared impatiently at the bland Eurasian. 'He will be 'hot', we daren't go near him until he has discarded the suit.'

Kerron nodded, and together they waited in the control room while the adventurer rid himself of the lethal radiation-soaked space suit. When he did enter the room he looked pale and ill.

'The tubes are cleared, and we can blast when ready.' He slumped down into one of the control chairs, the light from the uncovered ports striking flashes of living colour from his irillium garments.

'What were those things?' Kerron tried to control his impatience and failed. 'Did they harm you?'

'No.'

'The woman said that she heard voices from space.' Chang seated himself and stared at Brett. 'She is a mutant, is she also a telepath?'

'Yes.'

'Then what's this all about?' Kerron waved towards the drifting crystalline flashes of light. 'What are they?'

'The answer.'

'What?'

'They are what you wish to become. They are the immortals!'

'You're joking!' Kerron stared at the tall adventurer and felt fear well within him. He gripped the edge of the control panel, and slumped into a chair. 'How can you know what they are? Can you speak to them, question them?' Irritably he slapped the arm of the chair. 'Tell us, Brett! Tell us what all this is about!'

'Give me time.' Brett rested his head between his hands, and slumped with utter fatigue. 'You think that I'm joking don't you?' He stared at Kerron with eyes that held utter despair. 'I wish by all the gods that men have ever worshipped that I was, but I'm not, Kerron, I'm not!'

'Then explain! You said that those crystals were the immortals, but how can that be? They may have life, that I can't deny, not after seeing some of the life forms to be found on other worlds, but what of the secret, man? What of us?'

Slowly Brett straightened in the deep chair, his pale features lined and engraved with the marks of utter fatigue and despair. He rested quietly for a moment, staring at the splendour beyond the observation ports, and at the glittering ball of gold centred in the visi-screen. When he spoke his voice was dull and lifeless, the voice of a man who has lost all hope.

'What is life, Kerron? What is immortality? Did you think, as I thought, that it would be possible to live in a frame of flesh and blood forever?' He laughed, and the sound sent a ripple of fear through Kerron's withered body.

'How could it? How could we logically hope to reside for an eternity of time in a body as weak and as soft as ours? I am as immortal as any man can hope to be, my life is measured by the half-life of the radio-actives within my cells, a half-life of ten thousand years, but I am not immortal.'

He paused, and in the silence Kerron could hear the subtle whisper of cautious feet in the corridor outside the control room.

'Is stone eternal?' Brett shrugged as he spoke and frowned a little. 'Is metal? Is anything known to the mind of man? To be immortal a thing must last forever, and how can a man live so long? Flesh wears, bone, brain, skin, even the neural capacity of the brain must eventually be filled — and what then? Idiocy, and a welter of boredom, is that what you sought?'

Chang sighed, a ghost sound, and his yellow features were as bland as Kerron had ever known.

'A dream,' he whispered. 'A dream of fear and selfish hope. My ancestors knew better than we. They knew that immortality could only be attained through children, the handing down of racial memories and the continuance of the gene pattern from father to son.' He folded his hands, and the tears glistened wetly on his yellow cheeks. 'I have failed you my fathers,' he muttered. 'Unworthy am I of your love and care. Who now will continue the line and race of Chang?'

'You said that those lights, those

crystals were immortal,' insisted Kerron. 'What did you mean?'

'How old is the race of Man?' Brett still stared at the golden sun as if there had been no interruptions. 'Are we the first? In all the millions of years since life first began, can we say that we are the only race to have discovered science, the secret of the interstellar drive? If we can't, then is it beyond the bounds of possibility that other races have had the same dreams as we? The desire to live is strong, need we be the first to have tasted of that bitter cup?'

Silence again, and the soft breathing of someone lurking in the corridor just outside the room. Brett smiled, a smile of contempt for himself and for all men. It was not a nice expression.

'We are not the first,' he whispered. 'Once there lived a race of beings so great and so advanced in their science that we are as fumbling children against them. They solved secrets of nature that we only guess at, they set their foot on the universe, seeded planets with their children, and the race grew mighty and rose to the uttermost pinnacle of perfection. They reached the top, and they had but one direction left in which to go — downwards!'

Chang opened his lips, and closed them as Brett smiled pityingly at him.

'When a man has done all that he can do, when even his imagination fails to provide a spur to fresh effort, then that race is dying. It is a simple law, grow or die. No race, no individual, no living thing can do otherwise. Grow or die! Advance or retreat! Nature does not recognise status quo.'

'So the race died?' Kerron stared at the glittering stars and felt the nostalgia of a great sorrow.

'Yes. Not all of them, and not all in the same way. Some turned to battle, and the fury of their wars scarred space forever. Suns were drained of their energy, others exploded into novae, planets were wiped clean of life and left as bare rock and ash. Others rested, sinking deeper and deeper into decadence and decay, playing at what they once had been, drugging their minds and their bodies with lost and hopeless dreams.'

'The Lotus Eaters,' Chang whispered.

'A few solved the final secret, it is those few who appear to you as icosahedrons, twenty sided polyhedrons with each side a regular triangle. They are the immortals!'

'Impossible!'

'Why, Kerron? If you were to decide on a vehicle for eternal life, what would you choose? Flesh and bone? Remember that an accident could rob you of limbs, sight, a normal life. Would you like to be an immortal in a crippled body?' Brett laughed curtly as he stared at his own irillium covered arm.

'I know what I would do, and flesh is not the best vehicle, I know that too well. Metal and plastic? What good is an immortal robot? No, Kerron, the Elder Race knew better than we, and they chose the very basic material of all.'

'What is that?'

'Energy itself. Those polyhedrons are constructed of a wave-pattern of sub-etheric stress. They are not subject to material laws, they cannot be harmed by

171

any weapon known, bullets would penetrate them as if they were made of space itself. Energy beams are unable to affect the sub-space wave-pattern. They are immortal in every sense of the word.'

'How can they be?' Kerron stared at the glittering crystals flocking about the ship. 'I can understand how they could have been artificially constructed, but what of their life?'

'They are as alive as you are,' said Brett quietly. 'More so in fact. They see by the impact of a wide band of radiation on the outer wall of their wave-pattern. You must realise that I can only draw crude analogies, could you describe sight to a blind man? They see infrared, ultraviolet, a range of colours we have no experience of. They are mobile, by a subtle alteration of their frequency, they can nullify gravity, and travel at the speed of thought. They can penetrate solid matter, and by electronic control of matter, they can build, construct, and destroy. No, Kerron, rid your mind of the idea that they are helpless, they knew more of science than we dream of, and they built their new bodies with all the skill and cunning at their disposal.'

'How did you learn all this?' Chang stared accusingly at the tired figure of the tall adventurer. 'How did you communicate with them? When? Why haven't we learnt what you know?'

'Are you a telepath, Chang?'

'No.'

'Naturally the immortals do not use the pulsation of sound waves to convey meaning, they communicate directly from mind to mind. I am not a good telepath, though in the past thousand years I have trained myself to receive thoughts from an outside source. What I learned was transmitted by another, someone very near to me.'

'Nyeeda?'

'Yes. She is a mutant, a woman with alien blood and a different neural pattern to her brain. She and I are in constant rapport, and she acted as transmitter between myself and the immortals.'

'She could have lied,' said Chang quickly. 'How can you be certain that she did not broadcast her own thoughts?'

Brett pointed to the radio humped beside the control panel. 'If you were to contact another ship, and talk with their radio operator, would you trust your set, or would you fear that it was interrupting your conversation?'

'I would trust the set, naturally, but it is a machine, not a woman.'

'When Nyeeda acts as an intermediate transmitter she is also a machine, as much a machine as that radio. I cannot pretend to explain, some things just are, but I know that I learned the truth about those polyhedrons. If you heard what I did, then you could have no doubts.'

'We must trust you, Brett,' Kerron said quickly, 'but there is much to explain, so much to try and understand. What of us? Are we to die, or can we learn the secret of immortality?'

'I cannot answer that.' Brett stared down at his twisted fingers. 'The secret is not mine to give, and I do not know what will happen. They questioned me, robbed my brain rather, drained it of all knowledge. I sensed a certain hesitancy, a difference of opinion. They know why we are here, and the fact seems to amuse them.'

'Amuse them?'

'Yes.' Brett stared at Chang and smiled. 'Haven't you grasped it yet? What do you think inevitably happened when they warped space and locked themselves in a fold of the space-time continuum? The Wall remained unbroken for eons, they forced a rift in it and let the accumulated radiation stream out to the far corners of the galaxy. It was an experiment, the blast of hard radiation rekindled the seeds of life, and we are one of the results.'

'You mean that they deliberately locked themselves away behind The Wall?'

'Yes. What else could they do? For a while at least they were in doubt as to the success of their experiment and when they were sure, it was too late. They couldn't leave their prison, not until they concentrated sufficient force to blast a rift in The Wall. We came through that rift and here we are.' He stared at the two old men and smiled with sudden gentle understanding.

'Don't you see,' he said gently, 'we are

something new. Uncounted eons have passed since they became immortal, they have done all that they wish to do, and remember that they were a dying race when they took the final step. They were — bored, and we have given them a fresh interest.'

He smiled again and raised his voice.

'You may enter now, Forrest, there is no need for you to lurk in the corridor.'

Abruptly the door slammed open and Forrest entered the control room. He snarled at them, showing his snags of teeth, and dragged Nyeeda behind him with one hand She came calmly, her features calm and pale. She didn't resist though she was young enough and lithe enough to have quelled the old man with ease, but she seemed utterly disinterested in what the old bald-headed man was doing

Light gleamed from the slender barrel of a weapon as it menaced the tall adventurer.

12

Forrest's end

Time seemed to stop, to have no meaning, to rest and pause awhile before continuing its relentless progress. Kerron stared at the maniacal features of the old man, at the cold calmness of the woman, then in fascinated fear at the polished barrel of the weapon. Chang drew in his breath with a sibilant hiss, and Brett rose slowly from his chair.

'Stay as you are!'

Splinters of brilliance glittered from the pistol as Forrest jerked the weapon in an unmistakable gesture. He stared at them, a thin trickle of saliva running down his chin, and the expression in his hot eyes made Kerron feel ashamed that he had ever called this man 'Friend'.

'I heard you,' said Forrest. He sucked in his breath. 'You have found the secret, the secret of immortality, I know you have and I want it, do you understand? I want it!'

'Forrest!' Chang stepped forward and halted as the pistol swung towards him.

'Get back! I don't trust you, I don't trust any of you, you all want to rob me, to take my money and to keep eternal life for yourselves. I wouldn't do that if I were you, not if you want to live!'

Silence. Brett still sat calmly in his chair, his hands resting lightly on the irillium cloth of his knees. Nyeeda stood as if all that was happening was part of a dream, as if it were all utterly unreal and not worth the effort of trying to understand. Kerron stared at Chang, and the Eurasian licked his dry lips, then shrugged and sat down. By common consent all responsibility seemed to have been placed on Brett.

He seemed to be listening, to be only partly aware of what was happening before him, and the silence grew, each second increasing the tension filling the ship.

'You know what I want.' Forrest jerked his gaze over the little group before the control panel. 'I heard you talking. I want immortality, and I want it now!'

'You know of course that your ship was destroyed while attempting to penetrate The Wall.' Brett spoke as if he didn't care whether the old man heard him or not.

'What of it?' Forrest laughed and gripped Nyeeda's arm until his knuckles showed white and glistening against his cracked and sere skin. 'You'll get me what I want and get me back to civilisation — or the woman dies. Well?'

'What you ask is not mine to give,' said Brett calmly. 'I can tell you one thing, however, you are lessening your chances by the second. Drop your weapon, release the woman, and sit down.'

'Do you take me for a fool! I know how to handle you, Brett. Get me what I want, or spend an eternity mourning your lost love.' He laughed sneeringly and jerked the woman before him. 'Shoot if you feel like it, Brett, but remember what will happen to the woman.'

Silence fell again, a silence heavy with dangerous potentialities. Kerron glanced out of the uncovered observation port, and almost gasped with surprise.

Space was alive with flashing colour!

It came from the strange polyhedrons, hundreds of them milling and swaying about the immediate vicinity as if they were a swarm of bees clustered around a hive. They swung in intricate orbits, radiating brilliant surges of scintillating energy, red and green, blue and warm orange, white and murky brown. Even as he watched, more came appearing suddenly out of space, then more, then even more, his head reeled as he tried to follow the surging patterns,

He glanced at Brett, then at the woman, and finally beyond the uncovered observation port. He remembered what Brett had said, and tried to imagine what impact they were having on a group of immortals, beings who had not known an object of fresh interest for unimaginable eons.

Suddenly he understood!

He smiled and relaxed in his chair, Forrest glaring at him, and Brett watching him with a strange expression.

'You know?'

'Yes.' He smiled back at the tall adventurer. 'I know.'

'Relax and remain calm.' Slowly Brett rose to his feet, Forrest watching him and menacing him with the pistol.

'Sit down, Brett,' he snapped, 'Sit down!' With a sudden explosion of nervous energy he jammed the muzzle of the pistol against Nyeeda's side. 'Take one more step and I'll kill the woman,' he threatened. 'Don't be a fool, Brett! I mean what I say.'

'Ready?' Brett spoke to no one in particular, but slid his arms beneath the glimmering material of his cloak and deliberately raised his arms. The irillium spread, shielding Chang and Kerron with its spun metal, proof against a stray blast from the pistol.

'Ready,' said Nyeeda, and moved with a bewildering speed.

She spun, rolling herself around Forrest and striking at his gun, before he could adjust his posture she had slipped behind him out of reach of his pistol. At the same moment Brett stepped quickly forward. He lunged at the old man, grabbed at the weapon — and missed!

Forrest snarled with triumph, and stepped back, his thin finger tightening on the trigger. Energy spat from the slender barrel, a thin shaft of intense brilliance, hissing as it sped through the air, disrupting the sparse atoms in its path. It scintillated between them, stabbing from the unsteady hand of the old man and striking Brett directly on the flashing material of his blouse.

It splashed! Radiant energy sang through the air, singeing unprotected flesh and dimming the lights with the very brilliance of its passage. Brett grunted, lunged forward, and grabbed at the spitting weapon. For a moment he and the old man strained together, the maniacal strength of Forrest combatting the irillium weighted muscles of the tall adventurer. The gun spat again, a thunder of roaring destruction, and Nyeeda screamed, and screamed in sudden fear.

Brett sagged, clinging for a moment to the slumped body of the old man, then he straightened, and Kerron felt his stomach churn as he looked at the ruin of what had once been a face.

The blast had splashed from the irillium of the adventurer's blouse, spraying back in a swathe of destruction which had roasted Forrest's head from his shoulders, but had seared Brett's features with a kiss of flame. He staggered, trying to clear the rilling blood from his eyes, then slumped weakly on to his knees.

'Kerron! The medical kit, a nerve block, quick!'

Desperately Kerron filled a hypodermic and slid the needle beneath the skin of the neck. He pressed the plunger, and refilling the hypodermic, emptied it again in the great vein of the arm. Brett gasped, then as the luminous fluid blocked the pain sensations from his seared flesh, examined his face in a mirror.

'Brett!' Nyeeda ran up to him, tears falling from her wide eyes. She had lost her abstracted air, now she was all woman, and a woman mad with love and fear.

'It's all right, Nyeeda,' soothed Brett. 'Just singed a little, a hormone pack and regraft and I'll be as good as new.' He smiled at Kerron, the flesh wound on his face standing livid against the normal paleness of his skin.

'A good show wasn't it? Forrest did better than he knew.'

'Show?' Chang frowned at them, then took over the medical kit smearing the hormone quick-healing salve over the wound with surprisingly gentle fingers. 'What show?'

'What you have just seen. Kerron guessed, but said nothing. I knew that Forrest was waiting in the corridor, Nyeeda had told me what he intended. I thought that it would be a good idea to interest our friends out there.' He jerked his head towards the hull. 'They are bored, and we entertained them. That must mean that they are a little grateful, and if they are, we may expect that they will return the favour.'

'What can they do?' Kerron stared out of the observation port at the clustered polyhedrons.

'They know the secret of immortality, and that is what we came to find. If possible, I want to win that secret, for you

184

if not for others.' He stared down at the charred ruin of Forrest. 'A pity that he had to die, but his death was of his own doing.'

He stared at the distant golden ball of the strange sun, then at the surrounding orbs of vari-coloured light.

'Strange how the stars of this sector of space resemble an incredibly complex and vastly huge atom.' He tensed at a sudden thought, then shrugged and stared at the glittering polyhedrons.

'What happens now?' Kerron joined the tall adventurer at the port and tried not to stare at the ugly burn marring the hard features.

'We wait.' Brett pointed towards the glowing suns. 'Look, Kerron. All this reminds me of an atom, huge and complex to be sure, but still an atom. I wonder if it is one?'

'How could it be, the thing is too big, too vast, if it is an atom, what would it be an atom of?'

'I don't know, but how do we know it is so big? When we penetrated The Wall we could have diminished in size, become compressed in some way. The normal laws of our space-time continuum do not apply here.' Brett shrugged and turned from the port. 'Forget it, probably we'll know if and when we ever win immortality.'

'Do you think we ever shall?' Kerron tried not to sound bitter, but within him he felt the old fear. He would never see Earth again, he knew that. No matter what happened he could never live through the return journey, and if he did gain immortality, then he wouldn't want to. Immortality! He stared at the swirling polyhedrons with sick envy. They did not know fear, the helplessness of age, the horrible knowledge that was his. He had an agile mind, a young mind, he was far from senility, and yet that keen brain was trapped in an outworn body. He remembered the plans he had made when young, all the things he had wanted to do, and were still undone.

Now he would never do them.

Numbly he turned from the observation port and slumped in a chair. Chang sat beside him, drawn by a mutual sympathy and common sharing of trouble. Brett stood talking to Nyeeda, the murmur of their voices sounding strangely loud in the silence. Kerron stared at them, then at Chang. The Eurasian shrugged.

'Regret it, Kerron?'

'No, but I wish that it hadn't ended like this. Forrest dead, the ship almost wrecked, and us . . . '

'About to die?' Chang shrugged again and folded his arms. 'It comes to us all,' he murmured. 'We tried — what man could do more.'

Suddenly he cried out and pointed towards the glittering splendour of the visi-screen. Directly before them the golden sun loomed huge and mighty against the night space. Brett strode across the control room as he heard Chang's startled expression, and stared at the screen with glittering eyes.

'We've moved!' The Eurasian fought to regain his calm. 'I was watching the screen and suddenly that golden sun was as you see it. We moved I tell you, Brett. We moved!'

Tensely they stared at the screen and at the giant sun. Kerron stirred uneasily as he glanced at Brett.

'Shouldn't we drive into an orbit?'

'Wait.'

'We're too near, we may crash, get drawn into the gravitational field. Brett!'

'Wait I tell you!'

Tensely they waited, staring at the golden glory of the mighty sun, and as they watched Kerron began to lose his fear. He cleared his throat and pointed towards the visi-screen. 'Is that a sun, Brett? The instruments aren't recording heat or radiation pressure. It almost looks as if it is an artificial structure, a huge ball of some shining metal.' He stared frowning and narrowing his eyes against the glare.

'It *is* artificial!'

Suddenly the glow vanished from the screen. Without any sensation of motion, or of lapsed time, they had landed, landed on a smooth flat plain of golden metal. Brett grunted and turned away from the screen. Kerron ran after him and tugged at his sleeve.

'Brett, what has happened? Why are we here?'

'We're lucky, that's why.' The tall adventurer grinned as he stared down at the lined face of the old man. 'They have accepted us, the immortals I mean. I wasn't sure, couldn't be certain, though I'd hoped for this. They moved the ship, moved it to the centre of this space, to the birthplace of creation. Moved us to where the secret is to be found.'

'Immortality!' Kerron stared at the tall adventurer and fought to control the wild pounding of his heart. 'You mean . . . '

'Yes.'

Light splashed around them. Glittering light, streaming and flowing from a twenty sided polyhedron, three feet across and looking like a great and glorious crystal. It hovered in the control room, suspended at the height of a man from the metal floor, and even as they watched others came, penetrating the hull as if the sturdy metal did not exist.

Kerron cowered a little, shielding his eyes, filled with a mixed emotion of fear and awe, envy and anticipation. Brett stood tall and proud, Nyeeda at his side, and Chang remained as usual, utterly impassive yet with a burning emotion revealed in his eyes.

Forces surged around them, the half-felt, half-sensed flow of sub-etheric stress, and with the pulse of that strange power thoughts flooded their minds.

Kerron gasped at the alien sensation, and then remembering what he was and why he had come, straightened and stood proudly before the scintillating brilliance of the Immortals. He relaxed, forcing his fear to the background of his mind, and by so doing, losing his terror. He breathed deeply and carefully, oxygenating his blood and clearing his throbbing brain. He ceased to struggle against the wash of thundering thought-sensation, and instead tried to render his mind as blank and as receptive as possible.

Almost he could feel the satisfaction of the others surge around him.

Nyeeda gasped, then fell silent as Brett enfolded her with his arm. The tall adventurer stood limned with a brilliance almost matching that of the Immortals as the spun irillium of his garments reflected their light in a shimmering web of diffracted colour. He raised his head, the ugly wound stark against the sternness of his features, his eyes cold and grey as he stared at the hovering being.

'We are here,' he said. 'What would you with us?'

Kerron gasped, and almost fell to his knees as his head throbbed to sudden forces. He smiled, and the tears streamed down his cheeks.

13

Immortality

It was relief, relief and the sudden overwhelming knowledge that he had not lived or journeyed in vain. The glowing beauty of the hovering Immortal pulsed, and words came thundering into the hidden realms of his consciousness, first a single word, then others, but the first word was the one which had caused the tears of utter thankfulness.

'Welcome.'

'You know why we are here?'

'I know, and we bid you welcome. It has been so long since we have had contact with fresh minds, so long. You are welcome to stay. To become as we are, you and all your race. There will be struggle. There will be the clash of opposed desires and the strain of internal conflict, but this is well, for we are a stagnant race, and though we cannot die,

192

yet our minds can waste for want of effort. Therefore you are welcome, and when you are ready, we will make you as we are.'

'Thank you,' said Brett simply, and Kerron could sense his hidden emotion. 'I and my race thank you, and accept your offer.' He hesitated. 'Those with me are in dire need, they are old and are near to death. How long will it take to save their minds and spirits from decay?'

'A little time, a few breaths only. We need no machines for the conversion, not now, though at first the essential equipment filled this great sphere on which you stand. That was long ago, before we had gained full knowledge of the sub-etheric forces that we can now control. Are you ready?'

Brett looked at the others, and licked his lips. 'A moment. Does it matter to you?'

'No. Emerge from the ship when you are ready, we will wait.' Almost it seemed as if the glittering being could sense their emotion. 'It may be hard to bid farewell to the flesh.'

Abruptly it was gone, all of the glittering polyhedrons were gone, and they were left alone in the privacy of their thoughts. Brett sighed, and stared hungrily at Nyeeda.

'Now we part my darling,' he murmured. 'I could not love you in the flesh, for my touch would have meant your death, but love is more than the shape of your body, the touch of your hand. Together now we will live in imperishable bodies glorying in the harmony of mind and spirit.' He smiled down at her, staring into her eyes, then slowly he frowned and lost his smile.

'Nyeeda! What is it? What are you thinking?'

'Brett! Must we?' She clung to him, her eyes wide in the paleness of her face, and almost it seemed she trembled as she clutched at his arm. He smiled down at her and gently shook his head.

'Have no fear my darling, it cannot hurt and think of the future!' He stared at Kerron and Chang, his brows furrowed as he examined their expressions. Abruptly he laughed.

194

'I'd never have thought it, but why not? It is natural to be afraid, and yet what have you to fear?'

'I don't know,' muttered Chang. 'If I did I wouldn't be afraid.'

'I see.' Brett sat in one of the chairs and stared at them. 'You know the principle of immortality?'

'No.'

'Your bodies will be destroyed, nothing can save them and who would want to? Old, painful, almost useless, what good are they? No. Immortality does not depend on the flesh.' He smiled again, the sound of his breath sibilant in the heavy silence.

'It is your minds that will be saved. Your thought processes, the electronic surge and web of the wave-pattern which is the real you. Your bodies do not matter, cut off an arm and what have you lost? No, you are not the uneasy mass of flesh aging and wearing with time, that is merely the carrier of your brain, which in turn is merely the vehicle for the essential you. Save that, and you have immortality, lose it, and you are dead.'

He rose and took Nyeeda by the hand, smiling down at her trusting face.

'Come my darling, let you and I go together.'

'Brett!' Kerron reared up in sudden fear. 'Wait!'

'No. Come, Nyeeda.'

Together they moved towards the air lock, and Kerron wasn't surprised that it opened without loss of air. Gently Brett led the woman out onto the golden plain, walking as if they were a pair of lovers strolling across some terrestrial field beneath a summer sun.

Gently Brett pressed her to the smooth plain, then stooping over her, kissed her once upon the lips. He rose and gestured towards the distant heavens, the irillium covering his arm flashing and rippling with sudden colour.

Abruptly the plain glowed and scintillated with brilliant light. Three of the great polyhedrons, their twenty sided crystalline shapes blazing with radiant energy appeared out of the surrounding nothingness. They wheeled, spinning above the spot on which rested the woman, and the blur of their motion made a flashing circle of light defying the eye.

Faster they spun, faster, and then with startling abruptness stopped. They stopped, and where there had been three of the glittering polyhedrons, there were now four.

They hovered for a moment, then rose, darting towards the colourful glory of the glittering stars, and watching them, Brett raised one arm in final salute.

He stood for a long while staring at the distant stars, his shoulders slumped and when he returned to the ship, he walked as an old man walks, lifeless and utterly weary of life and all it contained.

Kerron ran to welcome him, and blinked unashamedly at his tears as he saw the expression on the tall adventurer's marred features.

'Brett,' he said, and swallowed at something in his throat. 'Why didn't you go with her?'

'How can I?' Wearily, Brett slumped into a chair. 'You must go, you and Chang, but I must remain.'

'Why? I don't understand, why should you be the only one of us all to refuse what you have sought for so long?'

'Must I explain?' Brett stared at Chang, and nodded. 'You understand, but then I believe that you have understood all along. I cannot go, don't probe, Kerron, don't merely satisfy your curiosity, isn't it enough that I must once again walk alone?'

'I'm sorry.' Kerron dropped his hand to the other's shoulder, and bit his lips. 'Believe me, I am sorry.'

'Better go now, Chang.' Brett held out his hand. 'I will meet you again, meet all of you, time and those who control our destinies willing. Goodbye.'

'Goodbye,' said Chang. He swallowed, and abruptly turned and strode away. Kerron watched him. Watched him as he strode out, on to the plain, signalled with one upraised arm, and settled down on to the smooth golden plain.

Still he watched, staring with hungry eyes as the glowing Immortals appeared, spun, then rose upwards towards the stars, now four where there had been originally three.

He sighed, and turned for one last look at the man who had done so much for all of them. He hesitated, then held out his hand.

'Goodbye.'

'Goodbye,' Brett clung to the thin withered claw and suddenly smiled. 'Forgive me, Kerron. I did not mean to be so abrupt, but what else can I do?'

'Come with me, now,' urged Kerron. 'Give up your struggle, take what you have earned.'

'No. Much as I would like to do as you suggest, yet I cannot.' He smiled at the puzzled expression on Kerron's face. 'There are twenty thousand people in deep-freeze within the vaults on Calistrana. Twenty thousand people who lie in suspended animation waiting for me to bring them the gift of immortality. Can I betray the trust of these people? There is a galaxy full of men and women who are cursed with the inevitability of death. I could lead those people here, show them the way, and open the path of eternal life to the race of Man. Can I refuse to do this?'

'You found the way here, why not let others find the same trail?' Kerron bit his lips as he realised the truth of what the tall adventurer had said. 'Tell others, your assistants for example, then return.'

'I intend returning.' Brett smiled and rose from his chair. 'What are a few hundred years when compared to immortality? What matter a thousand, ten thousand? I can do what I must do, and then return. You will be here to welcome me, you and Chang, and Nyeeda. Together we shall have fresh adventures, it won't seem too long.'

He walked out onto the golden plain, his arm firm about Kerron's shoulders. Gently he forced the old man to relax onto the smooth surface, then raised an arm towards the stars.

'Goodbye, Kerron.'

'Goodbye, Brett.' Kerron swallowed and tried to smile.

Colour swirled about him, a shimmering blaze of flashing brilliance spinning and swirling in an eye-twisting pattern. He felt a quick stab of fear, gone before it had registered and then . . .

Pain left him. The dull ache of bone and flesh and sinew. He felt alive, vibrant, quivering with vitality and the rushing forces of sub-etheric wave-patterns. He stared about him, and was not surprised to find that he could see in all directions. His vision seemed blurred and he did not recognise half of the colours he saw. Others swirled about him, and he felt the easy flow of friendly thought.

'Welcome. Now you must come with us and learn the use of your new body.'

'Thank you.' He allowed them to guide him, to help him as a mother helps her child, and knew that soon he would have no need of help. They rose, and to him it was as if he had merely thought of the concept of rising. Above, the stars shone with a new and intriguing splendour, and he felt quick impatience to be at work learning his new powers.

Up he went, higher and higher, then suddenly he halted, concentrating his vision far below.

A man stood there, a dot against the golden plain, the slender needle of a dull metal rocket ship resting beside him.

He stared, then feeling the quick surge of new forces hurtled upwards towards the stars.

Far below Brett raised an arm in farewell. Slowly he entered the ship and with a spurt of power, headed for the distant rift.

He felt very tired.

THE END